THE GHOST DRUM

THE
GHOST DRUM

A CAT'S TALE

SUSAN PRICE

Farrar Straus Giroux

New York

Ku pamię Leona Stanisława Hessa

IN MEMORY OF LEON STANISLAW HESS

THE GHOST DRUM

ONE

In a place far distant from where you are now grows an oak-tree by a lake.

Round the oak's trunk is a chain of golden links.

Tethered to the chain is a learned cat, and this most learned of all cats walks round and round the tree continually.

As it walks one way, it sings songs.

As it walks the other, it tells stories.

This is one of the stories the cat tells.

My story is set (says the cat) in a far-away Czardom, where the winter is a cold half-year of darkness.

In that country the snow falls deep and lies long, lies and freezes until bears can walk on its thick crust of ice. The ice glitters on the snow like white stars in a white sky! In the north of that country all the winter is one long night, and all that long night long the sky-stars glisten in their darkness, and the snow-stars glitter in their whiteness, and between the two there hangs a shivering curtain of cold twilight.

In winters there, the cold is so fierce the frost can

be heard crackling and snapping as it travels through the air. The snow is so deep that the houses are half-buried in it, and the frost so hard that it grips the houses and squeezes them till they crack. My story begins (says the cat) in this distant Czardom, on Midwinter Day: the shortest, darkest, coldest day, followed by the longest, darkest, coldest night of the whole year. On this day-night, this night-day, a slave-woman gave birth to a baby.

The woman lived with her husband's family in a small wooden house. At the centre of the house was a big, tiled stove. All day long a fire burned in the stove and sank its heat into the tiles. All day, and all night, the hot tiles gave their heat back to the house. At night the family spread their blankets on top of the stove, and slept there. With them, on the stove's top, tired and warm, the woman lay with her baby. Of them all, only the mother lay awake, as the night grew colder.

The slave-woman lay listening to the tiny sound, humming like the singing of a cracked cup, that the stove made as it breathed out its warmth. She heard the deep, sleeping breathing of the family around her, and the frost snapping about the roof.

'If only I had been born the Czar's daughter!' said the slave-woman to herself.'Then my baby would be an Imperial Princess and all her world would be warm, safe and rich . . . But I was born a slave's daughter, so my baby is a slave and she won't even own herself.'

That made her so sad that tears began to run from

her eyes. She thought, 'I have laboured like a she-donkey so my master, the Czar, can have another little foal to work and kick and sell as he pleases. I wish that neither I nor my baby had ever been born!'

Something struck the outer door of the house then. The door boomed at the blow, and the warm air of the house quivered among the roof-beams and round the walls. The slave-mother jumped with fright; but none of the sleepers near her missed a breath.

From outside, where the frost crackled, a throaty, rough voice called, 'May I come in? You in there! Say – may I come in?'

The family slept, unaware, as if the knocker at the door was in the mother's dream, and her dream only.

Another booming blow was struck at the door, and the slave-woman cried, 'Come in, and welcome!' For, who knew? It might be a traveller lost in the snow, and needing shelter.

She heard the outer door of the house open, and slam shut. Raising her head, she looked down from the stove-top and saw the inner door fly open. In hurried a tall figure, hidden under a big fur hat and a long, quilted, padded, fantastically embroidered coat. Bulky, beaded and patterned Lappish boots were on its feet, and large Lappish gloves on its hands. Over its shoulder was slung a flat drum.

This tall, odd figure crossed the room and climbed up to sit beside the young mother on the

3

stove. None of the sleepers woke. The stranger whipped off the fur hat, and the mother saw the face of an ancient woman, a face criss-crossed with wrinkles like fine old leather that has been crumpled in the hand. A thin beard of long white hairs grew from the old woman's chin, though her pink scalp could be seen through the white hair on her head. In the heat of the little house, the old woman opened her thick, padded coat, showing a tunic of leather beneath, decorated with beads and feathers. She pulled off her large gloves. She smiled at the young mother. Her few teeth were black or brown, with large spaces between them.

'A good night to you, daughter,' said the old woman. 'I've come a long, cold journey to congratulate you on the birth of a fine child.'

The young woman hugged the baby tight. This was a witch, come in the night as witches did come, to steal her baby and roast and eat it. She began to call out the names of her family, hoping they would wake her from this dream, or wake and drive the witch away; but they slept as if not a sound had been made.

'Daughter, my little one, don't be afraid,' said the witch. 'I've not come to hurt you or your baby, but to tell you this: the baby you hold in your arms is the child whose birth I have been awaiting for a hundred years.'

The mother opened her mouth softly, as if she would taste the witch's words. Her baby's birth expected for a hundred years? What was her baby,

4

then? A saint-to-be? Would there be candles lighting churches for her baby a hundred years from now?

'Give her to me,' said the witch. 'Let me raise her. Then she will be a Woman of Power, and the son of a Czar will love her. Keep her and raise her yourself, and she will be a slave and a mother of slaves, nothing more. Give her to me.'

The mother clung to her baby and shook her head.

'You see the Ghost-drum at my back,' said the ancient woman. 'You know by that I am a shaman. I can shift my shape and follow the dead to their world. I know all the magics, and am a Woman of Power, yet I was born a slave too. On the night of my birth, a shaman came to my mother and begged me from her. The shaman raised me as her daughter, and gave me a gift of three hundred years of life. For a hundred years now I have beaten my drum every day, and asked the spirits to tell me when and where my witch-daughter would be born. This is the night: your child is the child. Give her to me. In my care she will never be hungry or frozen or cruelly treated; she will not be a slave. Give her to me, and she will be free; she will have Power.'

Tears wetted the slopes of the mother's face and neck. 'I cannot,' she said. 'My baby doesn't belong to me. I am a slave, her father is a slave, and she and we belong to Czar Guidon. If I gave you the baby, we should be whipped for giving away our master's property. We should be executed for stealing from him.'

5

The old woman hopped down from the stove and hurried to the door, which opened before she reached it, and slammed after her. The mother heard the outer door open, and slam too; and she lay quietly in the dark, with tears running over her face, wondering if the witch had gone away.

But the doors opened and slammed again, and the witch came back. She carried a snowball as large as her head. She sat on the stove and shaped the snow in her hands, and it didn't melt.

As her strong, wrinkled hands, with their sharp, shifting bones, worked at the snow, the witch sang. Her voice travelled warm and humming through the dark, and seemed to set motes of darkness spinning. Lengthening, the notes of her voice rose into the rafters; and the young mother became calm and content as she listened.

The witch shaped the snow like a baby.

'Mine is a cold, pale baby,' said the witch. 'I have sung a spell into this snow, and even if you put it into the fire, it will not melt until summer comes again. When I have gone, and have taken my foster-daughter with me, you must show this snow-baby to your family and say that it is your baby's dead body. No one will be surprised. Many babies die in winter. They will take the snow-baby away and bury it, and no one will see it melt in the earth when summer comes. You won't be punished because a slave-baby died in a hard winter. Now give me your baby and take this one of snow.'

The mother brought her baby from beneath the

covers, but still clung and hesitated.

The witch laid her hands on the baby. 'Come; have sense and give her to me. Keep her, and you keep her enslaved.'

The mother released her hold on the baby, and the witch pressed it to her own chest, refastening her thick coat, so the baby was fastened inside. The cold snow-baby, the witch put into the mother's arms.

Then the witch jumped down from the stove, put on her fur hat and her big gloves, cried, 'I wish you well,' and rushed to the door. The door flew open, and the witch was gone through it. The young mother pushed herself up on one elbow to see the last of the witch, but saw only a closed door, and heard nothing more than the slamming of the outer door, and the crackling of frost about the house.

The snow-baby lay chillingly cold against her.

Before the night was over the mother couldn't remember if she had given her daughter to a night-visiting witch, or if the cold baby she held was her own baby frozen to death, and all the rest a dream.

So uncertain was she that she told no one about the witch, but only said that her first child, a daughter, had died a few hours after birth, in the coldness of a winter night. But all her poor life the woman remembered the witch, and hoped that she had been no dream.

TWO

At the end of its golden chain, the scholar cat walks round the oak and, as it walks, it tells this tale.

Did the slave-woman dream (asks the cat) or did a witch truly take her baby?

And, if a witch truly came, did the witch tell the truth, or did she take the baby, roast it, and eat it at a witches' picnic?

I shall think of the answers to these questions (says the cat) and while I am thinking, I shall tell of the Czar who rules this Czardom, the Great and Mighty, the Royal, the Compassionate, Czar Guidon.

Czar Guidon, that spindly-legged, spindly-armed, fat-bellied man, like a spider. That man who calls himself God on Earth, and who murdered all his brothers and uncles and cousins to make himself Czar. That wicked (but whisper this) wicked, wicked man, the Czar Guidon.

I shall tell of the Czar's sister, the Imperial Princess Margaretta, who dyes her hair blue and never says what she means, but lies all the time. She was a small girl when her brother murdered all their relatives, and so he let her live. Now he wishes he had murdered her too.

I shall tell (says the cat) of how the Czar found and married the woman Farida.

And I shall tell of Czar Guidon's son, the unfortunate, the lonely Safa Czarevich.

Now (says the cat) I begin.

The riches of Czar Guidon were beyond all counting, all reckoning, for he owned everything in his Czardom: every coin, every jewel, every crumb of soil and clod of clay; every mountain, every hill, every hole.

He owned every animal, wild or tame, alive or dead; and he owned every flower, every shoot, whether it grew in a wood, or in a field, in a garden, a window-box, a pot, or a crack in a wall.

If a bird or an insect flew over the border into his Czardom, then he owned it. He owned the air they flew in. He owned the air in the lungs of his people. He owned the people.

But he had no wife and no children.

The Czar's chair stood at the top of a tall flight of steps in the court-room at the centre of the Imperial Palace. The chair's back was like the spread tail of a peacock, covered with bright eyes of enamel and jewels. The Czar's advisers came and lay on their bellies at the foot of the Czar-chair's steps, and they cried, 'Oh, Compassionate Czar, do not punish us, but let us speak.'

The Czar nodded to his captain, who stood on the Czar-chair's lowest steps, and the captain stamped his foot as a sign that the advisers might speak.

'Oh, Compassionate Czar,' said the oldest of the advisers, 'we beg you, take a wife, and have children with her, so there will be a Czar to rule us in the years to come.'

This angered the Czar, but his anger passed, and he said, 'There shall be a bride-choosing.'

Among those who gathered in the court-room was the Imperial Princess Margaretta. Smiling, she stepped forward in her blue silks and blue sapphires, and she said, 'I am *so* pleased that my Imperial Brother is to take a wife. May I wish him, with *all* sincerity, a *very* happy marriage, and a dozen beautiful children to sit on his knee?'

All the courtiers politely clapped the Princess's speech, but not one of them believed her. Everyone knew that the Princess wanted to be Czaritsa after her brother's death, and if he had children, she would only have the trouble of murdering them. Everyone knew this: but still the Princess made her polite little speech and tried to sound as if she meant it; and still the courtiers applauded and tried to look as if they believed it. This is the way of Czars' courts.

But listen, (says the cat) the bride-choosing began.

Messengers were sent to every city, town and village, to every house and hut, in the whole Czardom; and the message they carried was: 'Every unmarried woman above the age of twelve must present herself at the Imperial City before the month is out. The Czar will choose a bride! Long live the Czar Guidon!'

The message brought sorrow to the land. Each family looked at their unmarried daughters or sisters and dreaded that they might be chosen to be the Czar's bride – a terrible thing, for Czars were cruel, and the relatives of Czars were crueller still. How long would the chosen bride live before being poisoned or smothered, or stabbed to death by the Imperial Princess? By slow carts, dressed in their oldest clothes, with their hair hacked short and ragged, all the unmarried women of the land made their way, from every part of the land, to the Imperial City. Their families wept for them, and prayed that the Czar would not like them.

In the Imperial City, hundreds of carpenters were at work, building houses where the women would live while the Czar chose from among them.

Hundreds of joiners made beds and stools and chests for the houses; and thousands of seamstresses stitched blankets, sheets, curtains and dresses.

Tons of food were brought to huge kitchens, where hundreds of cooks worked over hundreds of fires to provide meals for the women; barrels of water were brought into the city, for the women's washing, until it was said the rivers were dry.

Swarms of clerks wrote down the women's names, and the names of the places they came from.

There were thousands and thousands of women. Noble and slave-women; widowed women; old, middle-aged and young women; mere girls.

When the month was over, and every one of the

new houses was filled with women, the clerks went from house to house, inspecting and questioning them all. They were to decide which of the women could be sent home without even being seen by the Czar. They knew that the Czar wanted a pretty wife, but a clever one too, and they set tests for the women to pass: simple tests at first.

The women made the choice hard by trying to answer stupidly, to hide the skills they had. But the Czar was waiting, and the clerks were not over-long in making their decisions.

The next day, hundreds of women were sent home, a few in disappointed tears, the many in tears of thankfulness and relief. Back they went to their families and a happier life than they could ever have had in the Imperial City.

Those women who remained had to answer harder questions and pass stricter tests, sitting their exams in Czaritsaship. More of them were sent home; and the tests were made harder still. The clerks puzzled, argued, and made difficult choices, before sending home another hundred, and then another hundred, and another, until, of all the thousands who had come to the Imperial City for the bride-choosing, only one was left. That one was a young slave-woman from the south of the country. She was tall, dark-haired, dark-eyed, brown-skinned, beautiful and clever – but not so clever that she could be stupid. Her name was Farida.

She had been born in a small, poor house with

wooden walls and an earthen floor: now she was to be the lady of the Imperial Palace, which was as big as a town. A town of roofed streets which were corridors; of hills, which were stairs; of rooms as large as parade-grounds or market-squares, where fountains fell into marble bowls as wide as lakes.

It was dark in the Palace, even when it was daylight outside, because the windows were not of glass, but of fine, polished sheets of stone; and the stone was painted with the Imperial Eagle, and the Imperial Bear; with the Holy Golden Crowns, and the Flowering Tree of Life. Farida explored long passages, passing from a cloudily candle-lit gloom to a gloom turned golden and rich by light falling through the gold of the Holy Crowns; and then into an emerald gloom, darker and greener than that of any forest, and on into the rich blue and scarlet gloom of the Eagle.

Worse than the airless darkness of these corridors was the silence. No one spoke, not the guards nor the servants: talk was forbidden. Thick carpets swallowed the sounds of footsteps. This was the house of the Czar, the God on Earth, and only he was allowed to speak aloud without special permission. Servants and guards were whipped for making clatter. The Palace's silence was ancient and frightening.

It was all strange to Farida. She was given new clothes, taught to behave in new ways, and was not allowed to keep her own name. The day before her marriage, she was taken to the Imperial Chapel and baptized a second time. She was told that she had been reborn, and was no longer the slave Farida, but Katrina, the chosen bride of Guidon. To herself, she was still Farida.

Czar Guidon and Katrina-Who-Had-Been-Farida were married, Katrina was crowned, and the feast lasted three days. All the nobles of the Czardom were there, to swear loyalty to the new Czaritsa. The Imperial Princess Margaretta, dressed in blue silk, blue diamonds and blue sapphires, and with her hair freshly dyed blue, swore not only loyalty but love, to her new sister. She spoke with such sincerity in her voice, and such a look of true affection on her face, that everyone watching her knew that she wished the Czaritsa dead, and was already planning ways to kill her.

Many, many people pitied the Czaritsa, and none of them expected her to survive for long; but weeks went by, and weeks went by, and then the weeks were months, and still the Czaritsa was alive and, it seemed, the Czar loved her. At least he spoke to her pleasantly, and rarely kicked her. He had taken some thought to discover what she liked and what she disliked; and if some fruit, or flowers, or fine cloth were brought him, he would have it sent to her.

Even the Imperial Princess Margaretta took notice of this liking the Czar had for his wife, and laid by her plans of murder.

Then the Czaritsa's doctor went to the Czar and told him that his wife had a child inside her. An heir

14

to Guidon's Czar-chair, whether a boy or a girl, would be born in seven months' time.

Czar Guidon had married to get an heir, but now he was promised one, he was afraid. For two days he didn't visit the Czaritsa. He sent for his fortune-tellers and astrologers, and ordered them to foretell what the child would be, and how its life would run.

Now these astrologers and soothsayers could no more tell the future than the Czar could, though some believed they could. Those that did believe so went away to read the stars, throw the bones, scatter the sand, or whatever else they did while they made their guesses.

The rest called a most secret meeting in one of the Palace storerooms, to try to decide what would be the best and safest thing to tell the Czar.

What was it that the Czar was hoping to hear them say? The darkness of the storeroom was lit only by a single candle, and voices without faces spoke from the gloom.

'He wants us to say that his child will be as great a Czar as he is.'

'No!'

'We must say the child will be greater!'

'No, no! We must say the child will never be as great. That's what all fathers want to hear.'

'Not at all. Fathers want to hear their children will be greater than themselves.'

'If we say the child will never be as great, then Czar Guidon will execute us for calling his child a failure.'

'If we say the child will be greater, then he will execute us for insulting *him*.'

'What can we say?' they asked each other.

'Say the child will die young.'

'What if it doesn't? He won't forget what we foretold.'

'And what if it *does* die young? He will say we killed it by witchcraft.'

It began to be clear that whatever they said, the Czar would be displeased. Several of them left the meeting, packed their belongings, and ran away in the night. Those that remained at last went to their beds, dreading the time the Czar would send for them, but hoping things would turn out not so bad as they expected after all.

On the day the astrologers and soothsayers were called into the Czar's presence, they were sorry sights. One after another they tottered to the foot of the Czar-chair's steps, lay on their bellies, pressed their faces to the floor and begged for permission to speak. When permission was granted, they mumbled out whatever they hoped and guessed would please the Czar. None of them dared to look up at him. Many of them changed their minds about what they were going to say at the last moment. The child would be a girl – it would be a boy. It would be a great Czar or Czaritsa. It would quickly sicken and die. It would reign a hundred years.

Czar Guidon became calmer as he listened; and this alarmed everyone so much that the last few fortune-tellers could not croak a sound, and the place at the foot of the Czar-chair's steps was empty.

Into the space stepped the Imperial Princess Margaretta, carrying scrolls of paper in her hands. She looked into the Czar's face and said, 'Great Guidon, Czar and brother; these last years I have taken much interest in the stars and the ways they may be read. I have studied the best writers on the subject and, I believe, I am further advanced in the art of astrology than any of these wretches.' She held up her papers. 'I have made a horoscope for your unborn child, dear brother. It is rough, of course. When the child is born, I shall be more accurate, but this is as good a horoscope as can be made at present. Forgive my presumption, and allow me to tell you of it, Czar.'

Czar Guidon nodded his head.

The Princess unrolled her papers and studied them. 'The child will be a son, my dear brother; of that there is no doubt. He will have the beauty, courage and intelligence of his mother's people: in short, he will be a great man. The people will love him.'

Everyone in the court-room was peeping at the Czar. His face was white as plaster, and terrifying.

The Imperial Princess went on, 'The child's talents will make him ambitious. He will want the Czar-chair, and he will kill his father for it. Few will judge him harshly for that, however – you are hated, brother, and your son will be loved. It grieves me to tell you this, but the stars spell it by their progressions, and I know you value the truth.'

17

No one, from the most honoured courtier to the bravest soldier, could imagine how the Princess dared to say this.

It was a long time before the Czar was able to speak. His voice had to force its way past the fear and fury that filled him. In a scratchy whisper – but everyone in the room heard him – he said, 'Kill them, kill them. The astrologers, the fortune-tellers. Every one. Their heads – off!'

The soldiers left their places round the walls and herded all the fortune-tellers together. They were driven through the doors and, as they went, they broke the rule of silence by shouting out desperate pleas and explanations. There was no help for them. In the nearest courtyard, every one of them was beheaded.

'You my dear sister, my Margaretta,' said the Czar, 'you and only you tell me the truth, and the truth is what I love, above all. I shall reward you, my sister.'

The truth was that the Imperial Princess Margaretta could foretell the future no better than the astrologers, but she knew what it was that her brother dreaded.

Czar Guidon had never trusted his sister before, nor had he ever believed anything she told him; but he believed her this time, because what she told him was what he feared.

'Guidon, great Czar and brother,' said the Princess, smiling, 'if I have served you, I already have my reward.' She was sure that, because of what she had told him, he would have his wife and unborn child murdered. That was her reward.

But the Czar didn't have his wife murdered. The ways of Czars are not always to be understood.

At the top of the tallest tower in the Imperial Palace was a beautiful enamelled dome. Inside that dome the Czar had a little room built, and furnished with low tables and thick cushions. The Czaritsa Katrina-Who-Had-Been-Farida was carried to that room and locked in, with only one woman for company, a slave-woman named Marien.

Soldiers were set to guard the door of the tower, the stairs, and the door of the little dome-room. The Czar's orders were that his wife and her maid were never to leave the room, nor was anyone else to be allowed in.

The Princess Margaretta tried to visit the Czaritsa, but the soldiers would not let her by. She tried to send the Czaritsa poisoned gifts, but the soldiers would not deliver them. It was useless to try to poison the Czaritsa's food, for all the food served to the Czar and Czaritsa was first tasted by slaves who were specially trained to recognize the flavour of poisons. Those flavours could not be disguised from them by any spice, or any degree of sourness or sweetness. The Czaritsa was safe from everyone except her husband; the unborn baby from everyone except its father.

High in the little room inside the enamelled dome, the Czaritsa spent her days in grieving, and wishing that she had never been married. The maid, Marien, tried to cheer her with promises of how happy she would be when her child was born, but the Czaritsa said, 'How can that be? My husband is a cruel man, and he is angry with me. The Princess hates me, and would kill me and my child if she could. How can there be any happiness for us in the future? It would be best if I died, and the child with me.'

'Oh no, no, no,' said Marien. 'You must look on the bright side of things, Farida, little sister.' Marien and Farida were country-women and fellow-slaves, and they cared nothing for new names and new titles, but called each other by the names their parents had given them.

For long hours Farida would sit silent, trying to think of a way she could make the future happy for herself and her child. She hated the Czar, and did not think of the child as his at all, but as hers alone. When it was born, she must somehow escape from this tower and find her way over the wild country between this Palace and her home. She had no idea which way to go, but she would find it. And when she reached home, she and all her family would travel away into another country, out of the reach of Czar Guidon. Her baby would go with them, and would grow up, loved by its grandparents, its aunts, its uncles and its mother. It would know nothing of its cruel father.

That was her plan, and it was still her plan on the day her child was born. It was a boy. Marien wrapped him and laid him in his gold and ivory cradle. 'Let me rest awhile,' Farida said, 'and then I will take him home.'

Her rest turned to a fever, and within three days she died. It was Marien who named the child Safa.

The Czar Guidon knew neither that his wife was dead, nor that he had a son. No one dared tell him.

The news had travelled from soldier to soldier down the steps of the tower; and from the soldiers to the other slaves, and from them to the nobles and priests and the Princess Margaretta. Everyone in the Palace knew, except the Czar.

The eyes of the courtiers followed the Princess everywhere, hoping that she would tell the Czar. But the Princess was too cunning and said nothing.

Meanwhile the Czaritsa's body lay on the bed in the dome-room at the top of the highest tower, and Marien needed clothes, milk and toys for the baby. She begged these things from the soldiers, who begged them from their wives, mothers and sisters, but soon Marien said to herself, 'This is foolish. My poor sister must be buried, and little Safa will need new clothes as he grows bigger.'

She asked a soldier to step inside the room and watch the baby, while she went down the stairs, winding round and round, passing soldier after soldier. At the bottom, she asked to see the sergeant.

The sergeant sent her to a lieutenant, and the lieutenant sent her to a captain; and the captain sent her to the Czar's steward, who was in charge of all the slaves in the Palace.

'Will you go to the Czar and tell him that his wife is dead and must be buried, and that his son is born and must be provided for?' asked Marien, as she had asked the captain, the lieutenant and the sergeant.

The steward would not, but took her to the most noble of the Czar's advisers. 'Has the Czar been told of his wife's death and his son's birth?' asked Marien.

The adviser took her to the apartments of the Imperial Princess Margaretta, and of her Marien asked the same question.

The Princess smiled kindly. 'I shall myself conduct you into the Imperial presence of my great brother,' she said. 'You shall have the honour of being the one to tell him.' And the Princess rose from her chair, and herself led the way, on her own Imperial feet, through the gloomily jewel-lit, silent corridors. Slaves opened doors before them and closed them after them. Each pair of doors opened on rooms higher and larger and more painted and gilded than the last, until they reached the immense private apartments of the Czar, where the Czar lived in state like a flea in a cathedral. There the Princess, still smiling, left Marien. Her brother would be so furious at the news, she thought, that he would order the dead Czaritsa, the newborn baby, and Marien to be buried in the same grave.

The Czar lay on his bed, his Bible beside him. He looked at Marien and waited for her to speak.

Oh, how Marien wished she had not come! Now

she realized that her words might bring about not only her own death, but also the death of the baby she had taken into her care.

What words should she choose? What words would make the Czar loving and gentle?

She knelt on the floor, bowed her head and made herself as small as possible. 'Oh Father, protector of us all,' she cried, 'do not punish me for daring to speak to you. I have sad news of your wife, forgive me. She is dead, Czar.'

The Czar did not speak, and Marien did not dare to look at him.

'Father, dear Czar, be patient – I have come to beg you to give orders for the funeral, please.'

Crouched on the carpet, with her nose in its fluff, Marien heard the words of the Czar.

'She shall have her funeral, she shall have her grave. A small grave, but over it I shall build an Imperial Church. Every day and every night it will be filled with candles burning for her. A thousand priests will pray never-endingly for her soul.'

A strange grave, thought Marien, for a woman who had spent so many months in a tiny dome-room.

'Czar, be merciful,' said Marien, her nose still in the carpet. 'Be kind to me when you hear there is more news. Your wife bore a living child before she died. I beg you, let me have all I need for this child. Czar, Czar, have tenderness for your own child.'

'Is this child,' came the Czar's voice, 'a boy, or is it a girl?'

What did the Czar mean? Poor Marien's mind ran round in her skull. Did this mean he would be angry if it was a boy and pleased if it was a girl? Or would he be pleased with a son and angry with a daughter? Both sons and daughters can rule a Czardom after their father is dead; sons and daughters both can murder a father for his power. Marien rocked to and fro on her knees, striking her forehead on the carpet, weeping and wetting the rich, soft carpet with her tears. She did not answer the Czar at all, but only cried out, over and over, 'Be merciful, great Czar, be merciful, I beg you, I beg you.'

The Czar called for his captain of guards, and that silenced Marien immediately. In came the captain, with his long, heavy sword that could chop off a head at a blow. To the captain, the Czar said, 'Take this woman back to the Czaritsa's tower. She is the Imperial Nurse, and anything she needs is to be given to her. Carry the body of the Czaritsa to the Imperial Chapel. Ring the bells for her.'

The Captain saluted and dragged Marien to her feet by one arm. She was trembling so much that she could hardly stand, and once outside the Czar's apartments, she had to kneel in the dim corridors and cover her face with her hands while she gave thanks and waited for her heart to recover its normal pace and her legs their strength.

When she at last climbed back to the dome-room, the body of the Czaritsa had already been taken away, and the Imperial bells were already shaking the stones of their tower and shuddering the air with their terrible tolling, doleful sound, as they announced the death.

'Never mind, my sister Farida, wherever you are now,' Marien said aloud. 'I have saved your son. I myself went to the Czar, when no one else dared to go, and I saved him.'

She hopped about the room, hugging herself, and danced round the cradle, so pleased and proud was she. She opened the door of the room and boasted to the soldiers of how she had gone to the Czar and told him straight that he had a baby son, and should provide for him and bury his dead wife. 'You are a heroine, Marien,' said the soldiers. 'None of us would have done it.' And very soon the soldiers began to pass up the stairs well-cooked meals for the Imperial Nurse, good milk for the Imperial Baby, and beautiful soft clothes and toys too.

The dead body of the Czaritsa Katrina-Who-Had-Been-Farida was dressed in grave-clothes of red silk, sewn all over with gold and red stones. She lay in the Imperial Chapel of the Palace, circled round with burning candles that made her sparkle from dead head to dead foot.

The Czar personally chose the spot where she was to be buried, and set architects, masons and sculptors to work, to build a beautiful church over the grave. More sculptors were working on the tomb itself, which was to show the Czaritsa in Heaven with the saints, and was to be covered in gold.

From every district of the Czardom musicians and composers were being brought, to write and play the music that would be heard in the Czaritsa's church, and only there. Artists came, eager for the job of painting scenes from the Czaritsa's life round the walls of the church – a difficult task, for no one knew much about the Czaritsa's life before she had come to the Imperial City, and after she had come there, she had spent most of her days in one small, round room.

In the midst of all his plans for the new church, the Imperial Princess Margaretta came to her brother and said, 'In all your grief for the dead, my Czar, you are forgetting the living. Our poor, beloved sister's child is alive – have you seen the baby?'

The Princess knew, as everyone but the Czar knew, that the child was a boy, just as she had said in her lying prediction. When Czar Guidon discovered this, she was certain his fear would drive him to have the child killed.

'Our dear, sweet, dead Czaritsa – may God receive her soul! – would have wanted you to see the child,' said the Princess.

So Czar Guidon climbed the steps of the tower, round and round, past soldier after soldier, to the little room in the enamelled dome. The arms of the soldiers rippled like a wave as they saluted him, one after another. At the top, the last soldier roared, 'The Czar Guidon!' and threw open the door of the room.

The baby, Safa, lay naked on Marien's lap. She, who had been so full of how she had bossed the

Czar, was stricken utterly dumb by his arrival, and slipped from her seat to her knees on the floor. She could only think he had come to murder the baby, and she hugged it tightly and held it away from him – which was brave of her, however dumb she was struck.

The Czar stooped and took the baby from her. Marien gave one squeal and covered her face, thinking to hide from the sight of the baby's murder.

The Czar saw the baby was a boy.

He handed his son back to Marien and turned away. To his captain of the guards, he said, 'This room is to be guarded night and day. That child is never to leave it.'

The captain thought of how long the child might live, and said, 'Never?'

'Never,' said the Czar, and left the room. The arms of the soldiers rippled again as he passed. Not once, in all his life, did Czar Guidon ever visit that room again.

No one could understand why the Czar had not simply had his son smothered. It would have been much easier than keeping him imprisoned. Perhaps he did not want to put the idea of killing members of the Imperial Family into people's heads.

Czars were always hard to understand, though. No doubt, if the little Safa Czarevich lives to be a Czar, people said, he will be hard to understand too.

THREE

The cat walks round the oak, winding up its golden chain and telling its story.

Do you remember (asks the cat) the witch who visited a slave-woman and took away the slave-woman's baby?

What do you suppose became of that baby?

That is what I am going to tell now.

Do you remember that midwinter's night, when the snow was freezing to a crust of ice-stars? And how the old witch buttoned the slave-baby into her padded coat and rushed out of the house?

Out in the night, in the snow, stood another house. It stood on two giant chicken-legs. It was a little house – a hut – but it had its double windows and its double doors to keep in the warmth of its stove, and it had good thick walls and a roof of pine-shingles. The witch came running over the snow, and the house bent its chicken legs and lowered its door to the ground. The double doors opened, in went the witch, and the doors banged shut, one after the other.

The chicken-legs straightened again and lifted

the house into the air. The legs began to move. First they paced up and down on the spot, the talons on their toes raking through the crusted snow with splintering sounds of broken ice. Then the legs took a few quick, jerky steps, sprang, and began to run. Away over the snow ran the little house on its chicken-legs. Its windows were suddenly lit by a glow of candlelight. The hopping candlelight could be seen for a long time, shining warmly in the cold, glimmering twilight; but then the light was so distant and so small that it seemed to go out. All that was left of the little house was its footprints, the prints of a giant chicken. Snow fell and covered them, and by morning there was no sign left at all of the hut, nor of the witch who had taken the slave-baby.

The house bounded over the Czardom on its long chicken-legs until it was a thousand miles from any place where people lived, on the blank of a wide, snow-covered plain. Sky-stars glittered in the darkness above, snow-stars glittered in the white-ness below, and the long-travelling wind made its only sound as it blew round the corners of the little hut.

Inside the hut on chicken-legs was one small room, big enough for a witch and an apprentice. The stove, its door always gaping open, took much of the space, and the witch was careful to feed it often with wood and pine-cones, so the flames always burned high, and the room was never cold, nor the house faint with its belly empty.

There was a table and some stools, and a large cupboard where the witch kept her stores. The walls were hung with carved and polished lutes; with bells and drums and flutes; with psalteries and harps, and all other kinds of instruments for making music.

The witch could have lived in a far higher style, had she wished; but two hundred and fifty years before she had been born a slave, and she saw no reason to insult the memory of her parents by putting on unnecessary airs.

Now a witch has no time to waste in rearing babies, so, as soon as she had eaten, and built up the fire, the witch took down a drum and climbed on top of the stove with it and the baby.

The witch sat cross-legged, with the baby in the cup of her lap; she held the small, flat drum in one hand, and beat its tight skin with a bone. It was a quick, jumping rhythm that she beat, and in and out of it she sent her own voice, with a shout and a call.

It is easier to tell of singing a song than it is to sing it; and this song was a long one. It lasted a full year, and the witch often had to stop to eat and drink. She also had to move the baby from her lap, because the song made the baby grow.

Not at first; for the beginning of the witch's song was of all those things a baby learns in the first year of its life. Those verses sung, the witch called upon the baby's arms and legs to grow longer and stronger, and on its head and its body to grow, all in proportion.

It was a song with a strict and lively measure; and one in which there must be no mistake.

The next verses were of everything a child learns in its second and third years of life; and a call to it to grow. The witch took the little girl from her lap then, and laid her in blankets on the stove-top.

Verse by verse the song went on: long verses; a long song. But at the end of a year, when the song was finished, there was no toddler lying wrapped in blankets on the witch's stove, but a young woman of twenty years, sleeping and dreaming.

The witch laid aside her drum and flute and climbed down from the stove. She set on the table jugs of milk and bowls of butter, salt and pickles. She added plates of black bread and herrings, of sausage and blood-pudding; plates of hard, salty biscuits and dishes of soft cheese; a jumble of apples and sweet, wrinkled, long-stored oranges; onions, eggs, black pickled walnuts, apple cake, sloe vodka, lemons – in short, a plate or a dish or a bowl or a jug or a bottle of every kind of food and drink she had in store, until the table was so crammed that cups and plates were balanced half over the edge. The witch set all this out because, for a year, the little slave-girl (who was now a full-grown woman) had lived on nothing but magic, and, when she awoke, would have the appetite of a woman who hadn't eaten for a year.

When the witch woke her, the young woman came down from the stove and indeed she looked very thin, with arms and legs like sticks and a face so gaunt it was ugly. She sat herself down at the table and started to eat. For three days she did nothing – nothing – but eat and drink. Bread and more bread; cheese, pickles, vodka. A little fish, a little more; an orange, a sausage – her jaws never stopped chewing, her eyes never stopped darting hungrily about the table; her hands never stopped reaching for more food.

The witch left her to it, having work of her own to do, and, on the fourth day, the young woman's hunger was eased. Her face was no longer gaunt and ugly, though it still had a sharp look. The old witch paused by the table and its heaps of bread crumbs, walnut shells, apple cores and fish bones. 'You're welcome to as much more if you want it,' she said. 'What's your name?'

'My name is Chingis,' said the young woman. The old witch nodded, and left her to finish off what was left at the bottom of the bowls and bottles on the table.

The following day the old witch said to her apprentice, 'Now, Chingis, I have much to teach you and you have much to learn if I am to make you a shaman before I leave this world. Learn, Chingis, and become powerful: learn and I will reward you with three hundred years of life.'

'What must I learn?' Chingis asked.

'Oh, first, to be a mere herb-doctor: that is, to know the plants whose spirits heal and whose spirits kill, and to know that they are often the same plants. This should take you no more than a year, if you are as clever as I think you are, and pay attention.'

So Chingis and the old witch travelled from end to end of the Czardom in their house on chicken-legs, and they visited other witches in their houses, and hunted plants of seashore, forest, mountain and moor. They talked of the different plants, their shapes, their scents, the soils they grew in, and their uses; and Chingis stored such quantities of knowledge away in her head that she felt it must be growing bigger.

Other things were spoken of too.

'When you have been asleep, Chingis, has it ever seemed to you that you were awake and somewhere else?' the witch asked her foster-daughter.

'Yes!' Chingis said. 'I thought I was feeding a wolf snow from my hand. I was so sure of it, I felt the coldness of the snow, I felt the wolf's nose snuffle against my skin. But all the time I was on top of the stove asleep, and there was no wolf, and no snow.'

'Ah, you're wrong, Chingis. There was a wolf and there was snow. Only your body was asleep. Your spirit had crept from your mouth like a little mouse and run away into another world. It was there, in that other world, that you fed the wolf.'

'But I have seen many different places in my sleep,' Chingis said.

'When we fall asleep, and are dead to this world,' said the old witch, 'then the spirit that lives in us opens its eyes and goes wandering. There are a hundred thousand worlds it can wander in, some

33

like this world, some not. You must learn to know these worlds, and the ways to and from them. Never be afraid, little daughter, never be afraid, no matter how frightening the dream. It is another world and it cannot hold a brave spirit. A spirit cannot be hurt, and it cannot be killed. Back it will fly to its own body. You may even venture into the ghost-world, where the dead go and the unborn wait, and when you have explored *that* world, and know all the ways to and from it, then we shall call you a shaman. But hear this warning – listen now if never again! While you are in the ghost-world, do not eat or drink. Not one sip, not one crumb. If you do, you will forget this world, and you will forget the ways back to the other worlds; you will be as lost as the dead.'

'How will I know the ghost-world from the other worlds, Grandmother?' Chingis asked.

'Oh, you will know it. It is entered by a gate, a tall, wide gate, hung on such strange hinges that it opens any way you push it. If, in your dreams, you should find yourself before that gate, go through it, daughter, go through it boldly and never be afraid – remember the old saying: "Anyone who pokes their nose out of doors should pack courage and leave fear at home". But remember my warning too . . . Now, can you tell me the four hundred and fifty plants that heal?'

Through a long night, Chingis named and told of them all.

'Good,' said the old witch, 'and can you tell me of the ice-apple?'

'The ice-apple, Grandmother? I can't remember that.'

'That's because I've never told you of it,' said the old witch, laughing to herself. 'The ice-apple is rare. It grows in the far north, where no other trees grow. Northern summers have no darkness. The ice-apple flowers in the summer, white and brittle flowers that spread their petals to white days and white nights with never an instant of dusk. But the fruit of the ice-apple sets in the northern winter, when midnight and midday are as dark as each other. The apple grows and ripens – and is harvested – without ever knowing an instant of warmth or sunlight. An ice-apple is as clear and transparent as the purest clear-water ice.'

'Does it heal?' Chingis asked.

'She who eats an ice-apple will never be ill again,' said her grandmother. 'It would freeze her very heart. It would be to eat winter. Tell me, quick now, the plants that poison.'

Chingis knew them all. In less than a year she knew all there was to know of herb-doctoring; and the other witches they met, in their houses that ran upon goose-feet, or cat's paws, spoke approvingly of her and said they wished their own apprentices were as quick.

'Don't think you've done with learning,' said the old witch. 'Now the hard work begins. You must learn the three magics, and the first of them is word-magic. Everywhere you will hear the magic of words used – in markets, in Czar's courts, by family fires. Small children work tricks with words. You must learn all the tricks of word-magic.'

'Tell me some,' Chingis said.

'Suppose that a Czar or Czaritsa ordered their people to fight a war, a stupid war, a war that should never have been fought. Thousands of people are killed for no good reason, and their families left to mourn them. Much, much money is spent on cannons and swords, so there is no money to spend on other, better things, such as seed to grow wheat to feed the people – and thousands of people are cold and hungry because of this war. The Czar is afraid that if the people find out how foolish and wasteful the war was, they will be furious and do him harm. So the Czar uses word-magic. He says to the people, "The war was not foolish – no! It proved that our people are the bravest and best in the world because they died for us, and killed so many of the enemy. I know you are starving, my children," he says to them, "but that shows how noble you are and how willing to make sacrifices for the Mother-land. I, your Czar, am proud of you!" He says this and repeats it over and over again, and he makes his servants repeat it over and over to everyone they meet – and the magic works. The people forget to be angry. They grow *glad* that their sons and brothers were killed, and proud that they themselves are cold and hungry. This is the very simplest kind of word-magic, but it is very powerful, little daughter, very powerful indeed. Words can alter sight and hearing, taste, touch and smell. Used with a higher skill they

36

can make our senses clearer and protect us from the simpler magics. You will learn all this, Chingis, but you will never learn all of word-magic, even if you live three hundred years.'

So Chingis began to study words: the sound of them, the use of them, the shock, the smart and soothing cool of them. With her foster-mother, the old witch, she went to fairs, to markets, to cathedrals, to law-courts, to weddings, to funerals, where words and their magic may be heard flying.

Chingis was quick to learn the simplest word-magic, and could soon make anyone believe anything. And she learned to smell a lie, and to see the truth lying hidden under a liar's tongue. And no sooner had she learned that much than lessons in another magic began: the magic of writing.

From a chest the old witch took a book, opened it, and set it before Chingis so she could see the lines upon orderly lines of black shapes on the pages. From the wall the witch took a large, flat drum, a ghost-drum, and laid it beside the book. In the centre of the drumskin was painted an animal's skull and, round and round the skull, in circle after circle, in red and black, were painted more shapes, signs, symbols.

'Writing is another common magic,' said the witch, 'and the first step you must take in it is to learn the alphabet of this book, to learn what words these signs are speaking to you from the page. This is the simplest kind of writing-magic, but it is strong and not to be despised! When you can read this book, Chingis, the voice of a witch who has been dead two thousand years will speak to you from it. Every day, people who know nothing more of witchcraft, open books and listen to the talk of the dead. They learn from the dead, and learn to love them, as if they were still alive. That is strong magic.'

'What of the drum, Grandmother?' Chingis asked.

'That is a shaman-drum, a ghost-drum. On its skin you see an alphabet of a different kind. The alphabet in the book spells out words you can say; but the alphabet on the drum spells out things that can never be said. These signs on the drum are used only by shamans. With them you can read – and write – the movements of time, the thoughts of a fish, the moods that come and go through the heads of people without ever being spoken. The drum speaks these letters when it is beaten, and it speaks in the language of spirits. With this drum and its letters, you can read past and future; with these letters you can carve a spell in stone and throw the stone into the deep sea, beneath the waves, and the spell will last as long as the letters and the stone do.'

'This won't be an easy skill to learn, I think,' Chingis said.

'It won't be easy, and it is another art you will never cease learning,' said the old witch.

Chingis began; and had learned the simplicity of reading and writing the book's alphabet in a year. The letters on the ghost-drum were infinitely more difficult to learn, but Chingis knew that anything can be learned, with patience enough, and time enough. Slowly, she began to see in the black marks on silver birch-trees the writings of shamans and spirits. In rock grooves that seemed made solely by wind and water she found messages, curses and blessings, spelled them out, and was filled with eagerness to write her own.

The writings of spells is not for apprentices. Instead, the old witch taught her how to question the ghost-drum. A frail and brittle skull from some small animal – a mouse, a vole or a weasel – was set on the painted skull at the centre of the drum. Then the question was asked, and the drum was steadily beaten with the finger-tips. In skips, in slides and skitters, the skull travelled over the drumskin, driven by the vibrations of the drumbeat. On one letter it would rest a moment; another it would circle; some letters it connected by the straightness of its journey between them.

The drummer watched the travels of the skull with all attention. It spelt no words, but each letter gave meaning – though the next letter might change that meaning.

Either soon or late the skull would settle on a letter from which no time of drumming would move it. Then if the drummer had seen every movement of the skull, and had understood the meaning of the symbols it had touched, and had translated them into common words correctly, the answer to the question the drum had been asked could be given.

At last the old witch said, 'I can teach you no more in the magics of words and writing. From now on you must teach yourself in them. But I can teach you the last magic, the strongest and greatest magic of all.' From the wall the witch took a long-necked lute with a hollow belly of polished, ridged wood. She laid it in Chingis's lap.

Chingis drew her finger across its strings and a ripple of sound rose from the lute's belly through its round, pearl-edged mouth. 'Everyone on earth knows the power of music,' said the old witch. 'A village fiddler can play a dance tune and give all who hear new strength, though they have worked all day. And when their hearts are boisterous, then music can slow their hearts and bring them close to tears. A musician needs no words, spoken or written. Music is the language of the spirit that lives in us. Instantly the spirit understands, and understands all. But never forget how the fiddler has worked and practised, day after day, to learn the craft. You, my daughter, must work harder and practise longer, to learn a greater skill. Then, where the fiddler's music soothes, yours will heal: where the fiddler's music brings sadness, yours will bring sorrow, or despair, or death. Where common music brings laughter and dancing, yours will bring joy, or delirium, or even a shape-shifting . . . And when a shaman sets words to music, nothing in which a spirit lives can resist. When a shaman twines the two strongest magics together, all within hearing must do as the shaman wills.'

It is always easier to tell of a thing than to do it. In a minute I can say: Chingis learned all the magics so well that the old witch declared her an apprentice no longer, but a witch. Chingis's spirit came and went through a thousand worlds; and passed a thousand times through the gates of the ghost-world. She explored every sight and sound of that wide, forgetful land, and came hungry back to her body and her witch-mother – to be declared a shaman. In a minute I can say all this, but it took Chingis years to accomplish.

But once accomplished, what triumph! From every part of the world came huts walking on ducks' feet, bears' feet, donkeys' feet, bringing witches and apprentices to congratulate the old witch on her pupil's success. Far from any town or village, lost on the snow-covered plain, the houses met, and the witches came together and embraced and feasted and cheered Chingis as a new member of their order, and one destined to be great among them.

But there was one witch who did not celebrate the end of Chingis's apprenticeship. This was Kuzma, who lived in the far north and had never left it. He was the harvester of the ice-apples.

Kuzma was always alone, and he was often lonely, yet he would not leave the north. Instead he used his drum and his brass mirror to spy on the rest of the world and, alone in his hut in the far, cold north, he would laugh at the things he saw.

But when he looked into his mirror and saw the celebrations for Chingis he didn't laugh. He heard the laughter of others, and he heard their compliments to Chingis, and their praise of her, and he hated the sounds because they weren't for him.

He took his drum and questioned it concerning Chingis; and the drum told him that if Chingis lived out the three hundred years her foster-mother had given her, she would be a Woman of Power and a far greater shaman than he could ever hope to be, though he was two hundred and sixty years old already.

And Kuzma swore that if he could do Chingis harm, then he would.

FOUR

The scholar-cat tells its story to the chink of its golden chain.

Forget Chingis and her witch-mother for a little while (says the cat). But remember Kuzma, the harvester of ice-apples.

Best of all, remember the woman Marien and the baby Czarevich whose life she saved. Remember how the baby's father, the fearful Czar Guidon, gave orders that the Czarevich was never to leave the tiny room in which he had been born - that tiny room at the very top of the Palace's tallest tower.

Now I shall tell how Safa Czarevich lived and grew in that little room, under the care of the slave-woman, Marien.

The room was round, with round walls and a round ceiling and steps leading down to its locked door. It had no windows, and was always gloomily golden from the hot light of candles and oil-lamps. And, poked high, high above the silence of the Imperial Palace, it was full of the squealing of the baby and the singing of the nurse.

Every day soldiers carried tall wooden churns of

milk and water up the stairs, and left them just inside the door of the dome-room. They brought meals from the Czar's kitchens for Marien, and took away her empty dishes. Night and day they guarded the stairway, and allowed no one to pass up and down it except Marien. Even when the Princess Margaretta came herself, 'to visit her little nephew' as she said, the soldiers crossed their pikes across the steps and would not let her pass. They were afraid to look at her, or to speak to her, but she might not pass – not until she was Czaritsa.

Marien often ran down the stairs, rapidly whirling by soldier after soldier – and, a few minutes later, she would breathlessly run up them again, round and round. She could not bear the close, cramped, dim room, and she scuttled to escape it: but she could not bear to leave the baby alone either. Every moment she spent in the long, silent stretches of the Palace corridors, or out on the wide, fresh, brilliant Palace lawns, were plagued by the fear that, somehow, the Princess Margaretta was reaching the baby, like a cat that would smother him. Marien even imagined the Princess climbing the walls of the tower and biting her way into the dome through its enamelled bricks. She imagined the Princess creeping past the soldiers unnoticed, by witchcraft. She imagined the Princess with knives, with poison, with savage wild animals to eat the baby. And back to the room Marien would run, up all those stairs, reaching the top in an agony of breathlessness to find one of the soldiers poking the giggling baby in the belly, or holding him safely above his head in one hand and making silly noises.

The baby grew quickly – one month, two, three . . . One year, two years . . . And still the tiny dome-room seemed a large and interesting place to him, as he crawled and toddled over the expanse of the bed, mountained as it was with heaps of bright cushions. He tumbled the cushions and sheets about in search of his toys, and examined each pictured tile on the stove, and each embroidered scene on the cushions and wall-hangings. Marien told him the names of the things he saw. This stripey toy was a tiger, and this spotty one a cow. This flat, silk-stitched thing was a tree, with flowers on its branches, and here, painted blue on a white tile, was a ship on the ocean. This little wooden thing that looked so like Marien was a woman. Another wooden toy Marien said was a man, like the soldiers, but it didn't look much like the soldiers, having no overcoat and no pike. Safa decided that soldiers were soldiers, and that men were something he had not seen yet.

There were a thousand things he had not seen yet. Marien told him stories about knights and their horses of power; about forests and rivers, about fire-birds and singing-birds and princesses, who were always beautiful and truthful.

To Safa, the forests were like the embroidered forests on the cushions - immensely tangled with huge, silken, green leaves, yellow stems and flowers of sequins and pearls. He didn't know what birds were, but he knew what fire was, and through his fantastic embroidery forests flew flames that sang as Marien sang. The princesses were all like Marien, beautiful and truthful, and the knights were all like the soldiers, riding on stiff-legged, clumping wooden horses over carpet plains where wooden cows were hunted by wooden tigers.

In the middle of shuffling his toys about, the little Czarevich would stop and stare; and his eyes would be lit by the glow of the pearl and silk forests and the flame-birds in his head.

He began to understand that these things Marien told him of were on the other side of the door.

A short flight of white stone steps led down from their room to a tiny landing and a big, solid, polished wood door. It was always locked. On its other side stood the soldiers, on guard.

Sometimes Marien would open the door and a soldier would come in. The soldier would pick Safa up and talk to him, pretend to eat him, tickle him, put him on his shoulders and ride him round the room – but Marien would have gone, slipped away to the other side of the door.

The door would slam shut when she came back. Up the white steps she would come running, her face red and wet with the heat of her hurry. She would snatch Safa from the soldier and hug him too tightly, hurting him. Down she would sit with a thump, still grasping him tightly, kissing him and panting, 'I'll never let them hurt you, I never will, never.'

46

Safa thought she was talking about the tigers who lived on the other side of the door. She had told him what ferocious beasts they were.

Soon, whenever a soldier came into the room, Safa would run to Marien and beg her to take him to the other side of the door too. Instead, she lifted him and put him into the arms of the soldier, and promised to be back soon.

Safa would then scream and struggle in the soldier's arms, and though the soldier jounced him in the air and whirled him round, and held him upside down by the ankles, he would not be distracted or amused, but yelled all the while for Marien.

When Marien returned, she found the soldier irritable and Safa exhausted and whimpering. He wanted to know where she had been, and she tried to tell him about the Palace kitchens, and the lawns and rosebushes – with the result that, for days after, he begged her incessantly to take him to the other side of the door, and show him the roses, the grass and the kitchens. He had no idea what any of these things looked like, and for that reason he wanted to see them inordinately.

Marien longed to give way to him, but dared not. It would have been a pleasure to her to show him these things for the first time - but something very far from pleasure might result if the Czar were reminded of his son, or if the Princess Margaretta were to come upon the little Czarevich in some quiet part of the garden where he had run alone. In the dome-room he was safe. This Marien explained to him, saying that it was not permitted for him to see the other side of the door; he could not and he must not.

This made no difference to Safa. Please, please, Marien: he wanted to see where the water came from. He wanted to see forests (sequin-flowers glimmered in his imagination). He wanted to see real horses and talk to them.

'No!' Marien shouted in desperation. She picked up a wooden tiger and made it charge at him through the air. 'You know how fierce tigers are. They are big and strong, with big teeth, and they live on the other side of the door.' She made the tiger jump at his shocked little face, and he flinched. 'If I take you outside, they will come rushing at us and eat you. They like little boys' soft flesh.' She snapped her teeth at him, and he saw himself being eaten by a tiger, just as easily as Marien would eat a chicken leg.

'I'll hit the tigers,' he said, much afraid.

'Hit the tigers? They are bigger and stronger than – than the soldiers!'

He gasped; and was so afraid that, for a few hours, he stopped asking to be taken outside the room. But then he came sidling up to Marien and pushed into the folds of her skirt, leaning against her legs. 'We can run away if the tigers come, Marien. We can shut the door and they won't be able to get in.'

She snatched him into the air and held his face to

48

hers. 'Oh, but the tigers would see you and know you were here. They would chew down the door and eat us both.'

Safa's dark eyes showed white all round and he trembled. 'The soldiers wouldn't let them!'

'The tigers would eat the soldiers! Overcoats, buckles, belts and all!'

Then Safa knew the full terror of tigers, the fearsome strength of their jaws and bellies. When Marien put him down, he lay quietly on the cushions. For a week he did not ask to be taken from the room, but he lined up his wooden tigers, and killed them again and again.

The next week he crawled into Marien's lap and hugged her neck in his short little arms, kissed her and said he loved her until she was so silly with fondness she would have done almost anything for him. Then he said, 'If the soldiers go with us – and if we watch all the time for tigers – and if we run away fast when we see the tigers coming far off – can we go to the other side of the door, please, Marien?'

Marien roughly pulled his arms from her neck, shook him spitefully and pushed him away. 'I've told you, you can't leave the room! If you ask me again, I shall beat you! Naughty boy! Go and stand by the wall and cover your face, bad, bad boy!'

Safa was shocked by her unreasonableness and stood with his hands over his face, sobbing. Poor Marien turned her back on him, for she was crying too.

Marien went to the captain of the soldiers and

asked if leaves and flowers could be brought for the Czarevich to see; and perhaps a caged bird and a kitten. But the captain was not well that day – at least he was in an irritable mood and wanted to be unpleasant to all about him.

'Under no circumstances,' he said. 'My orders were to see that you had everything necessary. Flowers, leaves, cats – you don't need these things. It's out of the question.'

The more Marien argued, the more pleasure the captain took in refusing her. And when his bad mood had passed, and he would have liked to send potted trees, bouquets, sprays of leaves, to the Czarevich, he could not, because he could not go back on his own orders.

And so, to try to pacify the angry little boy, Marien had to go without her walks in the palace gardens, and shut herself, for all of every day, in the tiny round room, which seemed drearier and smaller as time went on. Nor did Safa ever forget that there was another side to the door, and he began trying to reach the other side by himself.

The door was locked, and he had, therefore, to wait until it was opened. Then he would make a rush – and be caught and lifted from his feet by a soldier and carried back inside. He glimpsed a landing, almost dark, and strange shapes of more soldiers in the further dark; and that was all. The whole world, it seemed, was roofed and walled and almost dark. Why did Marien talk about bright daylight, and space that had no walls? Did she invent these things? He could never be sure, and was for ever tantalized by the feeble efforts of his imagination to show him these unknown, unseen things. Every day he crept down the steps to the door, to wait for the door to be opened. Every day he quarrelled with Marien, who did not want him to wait there. And the soldiers had learned to expect his rush, and guarded the door so well that he never got further than the threshold.

Time passed by; the Czarevich grew bigger. He looked up at the overhanging, curving ceiling, which curved down and became the round wall, enclosing him as if he lived inside a nut. No windows. What was on the other side of this wall-ceiling, this ceiling-wall? Was there nothing on its other side? And what did nothing look like?

The Czarevich climbed the hangings on the wall, trying to reach the summit of the dome where – who knows? – there might be another door. His climbing tore the hangings in shreds, and then he climbed them simply to rip them.

He tried to batter a way through the walls, and broke many toys and bruised himself. He leapt on Marien's back and would not be dislodged, yelling that she must take him to the other side of the door, now, now! When she hit him, he hit her back.

Outside, the short summer was passing into the long winter. Marien knew it, and hated to be shut away from all knowledge of the sun's warmth. She was seldom loving any more; seldom told stories, but yelled and slapped.

There were long, dark days when she and Safa hated each other, and it was as if the little dome was packed with harsh noises, and thorns and barbs that scratched and annoyed; that exhausted them and made their heads ache.

But still Marien was afraid to do or say anything that would bring Safa to the notice of his father again. She was sure that the Czar had forgotten them, and that was why they were still safe. Orders had been given to the kitchens and the soldiers, and those orders would go on being obeyed for years without the Czar ever having to think about them. If the Czar was reminded of his son, everything might come to an end.

Safa Czarevich went on growing. He ran and jumped, even though the room was so small that his leaps took him crashing into the walls and into Marien. He ran round and round the circling walls until he was too giddy to stand, howling until the dome vibrated; he would throw himself down on the cushions, roll, spring up and rush at the wall with a yell; and run round and round again. Marien was distraught. She longed to walk on the lawns with space and quiet about her. I must, I must do something, she said to herself. I must go to the Czar.

But the soldiers brought her gossip of executions, and always she thought it best to wait a little longer. For another year she endured, always believing that she could stand no more of it; and for yet another year after that.

Safa grew. His running and whirling filled the

dome; and still he was determined to see what lay outside. Still he begged and pleaded, shouted and demanded, to be taken to the other side of the door. Now he fought with the soldiers.

By degrees Marien was pushed towards her decision. Every day she promised herself that *this* was the day she would go to the Czar. But then she would rethink matters and see that things weren't so bad as she had supposed. By the end of the day she would be so exhausted that she would make up her mind anew. *Tomorrow* she would go to the Czar.

With each new determination she was a little more determined, until there came the day when she went behind the screen, washed and changed, and, despite Safa's anger, got out of the dome-room. Down and round the stairs she ran, hearing the screams of Safa behind her.

Even then she stopped and wondered, and almost turned back; but no; she had come this far.

She did not waste her time on the soldiers, but went straight to the Palace steward. It did her no good. The steward was too clever a man to be responsible for reminding the Czar of his son, and he sent Marien away.

She went to the Czar's chief adviser, who was also too clever to help her. 'The time is inconvenient to speak to the Czar on this head,' he said, knowing he might lose his own if he did.

'Well, it seems that I must go to the Princess Margaretta,' Marien said, and to the Princess she went.

The Princess had her admitted to her apartments at once. Of *course* she remembered the nursemaid, and she listened with such a sweetly worried expression to all that Marien told her. She *quite* understood the nurse's anxiety; she realized *very well* what a miserable existence it must be in the dome. She herself considered the orders given by her great brother to be quite *mistaken*. And of *course* she would ask her brother to see Marien. Of *course* she would give Marien all the help she could. 'Why, there are apartments close to mine the Czarevich could have. Wouldn't that be *delightful*?'

Smiling kindly, the Princess led the way through the corridors to the grand court-room where the Czar was busy with his courtiers and advisers.

Oh, thought Marien as she walked behind the Princess, you are so smug because you think harm will come to my little Safa and me through this – but I'll show you! The Czar listened to me last time, and he'll listen again.

They reached the carved double doors of the court-room, all gilded and shining dully in the candlelight of the corridor. In the shadows on either side stood armed soldiers. They opened the doors for the Imperial Princess and closed them after her, shutting Marien outside.

A long unhappy wait. Then the doors were opened again, and Marien looked down the length of an immense room, hardly more brightly lit than the corridor. At either side of it stood crowds of people, their clothes darting out the subdued light of the jewels they wore, their faces all turned towards her in amusement. From them to her, carried on the draught of the opening doors, came a scent of powder and lavender; of musty roses and waxen candles burning. At the end of the corridor these people made, far away, was a high flight of steps; and, at the top of the steps, the most brightly lit thing in the room, was the Czar-chair with its gorgeous back like a peacock's tail. On the Czar-chair, looking down, sat the Czar to whom she must speak.

Marien started into the room and walked between the tall rows of courtiers. She looked at nothing but the steps leading to the Czar-chair. Her wooden shoes clacked and clapped on the tiled floor, and the courtiers sniggered.

She reached the steps of the Czar-chair, and crossed her arms on her breast and bowed her head low. In the proper manner, she went to her knees, touched her forehead on the first step, and called out, 'Do not punish me, Father, but let me speak!'

The captain of the Czar's guards stamped his foot to tell her that the Czar had given his permission.

Marien saw marble steps shining faintly green in the dim light, and a purple carpet that seemed black. 'Czar,' she shouted, 'I have come to remind you that you have a son!'

Every sound – of hair rustling on collars, of shoe-soles squeaking tinily on tiles, of breath shushing in throats – stopped. Marien's heart beat like a drum-roll, and rattled in her breast; but what was there to do but go on? 'Czar, your son cannot read or write; he is ignorant of everything and as unruly as an untrained dog. How is he to be Czar after you if he never leaves the dome-room? Czar; what are you going to do for your son?'

Marien never looked higher than the steps before her, so she did not see the Czar beckon to his captain. She started and raised her head, however, as the captain ran past her up the steps with his sword clattering on its harness at his side. Right to the top of the steps, to the throne-chair itself the captain ran, and bowed his head to the Czar's mouth. Then the captain straightened, turned to the room, and shouted orders in a voice so loud and high that Marien didn't know what he had said.

A soldier came to either side of her and squeezed her arms in tight, hard grips. They lifted her up and moved her away before she could begin using her legs for herself. Her head turned – she looked over her shoulder and all about, her face bewildered and afraid – and all the faces she saw looking back at her were afraid too, all those great, grand people – they were also terribly afraid.

Out through the gilded doors into the corridor she was carried. She didn't know what was going to happen, and she didn't struggle or ask questions. Swiftly, she was brought into the dazzling light of a small courtyard, open to the sky, and there – when the soldiers' eyes had grown used to the light – they cut off her head.

The rooms and corridors of the Imperial Palace

were always dark, filled with the frail, gauzy half-light of candles and painted windows; their corners piled with deep shadows. The rooms and corridors were always silent – silent for hours upon hours, and then disturbed only by the scratchiest and thinnest of whispers.

As night came, candles in the least used corridors would be allowed to burn themselves out; and those passages, those rooms, would vanish in utter darkness, utter quiet. The darkness and quiet crept through the Palace, making a silent, blotting leap to swallow a court-room emptied of courtiers; following the Princess to bed and the servants from the kitchen. At the deepest hour of the night the only faint smears of light were to be found where soldiers stood on guard – at the doors of the Czar's and the Princess's apartments; at the Palace gates; and on the steps of the highest tower.

In the dome-room at the top of the highest tower the candles had burned out, and even the smell of burning they had left had faded. In the darkness Safa Czarevich sat awake, waiting the return of Marien, his nurse. All the night passed over his open eyes, and Marien didn't come.

The morning light shone through the painted stone windows of the Palace, letting a many-coloured twilight of deep shadows into the rooms and passages. Servants walked silently, lighting candles which glowed in the dusk. But, high above the Palace, in the dome-room, where there were no windows, and no one to light candles, there came no new light. Safa waited in the continuing darkness.

The soldiers coming on duty and taking the place of the night-guards didn't speak, but Safa heard the dull tramping of their feet on the stone steps outside his room. He pressed to the door and called out for Marien. She didn't answer, but a soldier struck the door and said, 'Your nurse has gone away.'

In Safa's mind the world was the dome-room and the landing outside it. Where could Marien have gone? She was on the other side of the door, without him.

He waited, sitting cross-legged among the cushions. The door opened, and he thought she had come; but soldiers entered bringing food, water and lantern-light. They found fresh candles and lit them. Safa's sight returned from the darkness, and he looked carefully and saw that Marien wasn't among the soldiers.

'Where is she?' he asked.

The soldiers were leaving the room. One looked back and said, 'She's never coming back, ever.'

Safa had no understanding of 'never' or 'ever'. He thought the soldier was telling him to be patient and wait a little longer.

So began the years the Czarevich spent alone. His father the Czar had ordered the execution of the Imperial Nurse, but he had given no orders regarding his son. So the soldiers went on guarding the tower, and food, candles and fuel continued to be carried up the long staircase. These things would go on and on, and never stop, so long as there was a palace and a Czar.

At the beginning of this time the soldiers would speak to Safa through the door, or stay with him a while when they brought in his food. But Safa wanted to see what was on the other side of the door, and he wanted to find Marien. He rushed at the soldiers when they opened the door, and tried to force his way past them. They pushed him back easily, so Safa became more cunning, and wild. He would let them come into the room, and then attack them suddenly, with hard blows from his fists, or any weapon he had – a candlestick, a bowl, a jug. The soldiers were angry. They flung him bodily on to the low bed, to give themselves time to escape, and Safa would laugh uproariously, hilariously, at his own, half-expected failure. The loudest noise in the Palace was his laughter.

The soldiers grew afraid of him, and said he was mad. They retreated to their side of the door, and locked the door and kept it locked. Up the stairs they brought a carpenter of their regiment who – despite much interference from the Czarevich – succeeded in making a small hatch in the door, through which food and water and firewood were passed. After that the soldiers needed only to enter the room once a year – to light the stove for winter.

The rest of the time they guarded the staircase and the door, and kept quiet when Safa called out to them from his darkness. In time, he stopped talking to them, though they often heard him talking to himself, shouting aloud and running about the room, smacking into the walls. And then, for days on end, he would be silent.

Silent, in the darkness, Safa tried to force his mind to show him the other side of the door, where Marien was; but he could only imagine what he had already seen – round, walled places, wooden animals, sequinned vines, candlelight.

His body was imprisoned, but the spirit that lived in him, and was his thinking, strove until it ached, strove to leave the dome-room; and its fury made his body ache, at his heart, because his spirit was so firmly rooted there.

Even in dreams his spirit could not see beyond the dome's walls. It knew no way out of the dome.

But all night long – and all day too – this spirit made a long, shrilling calling – a high, unheard note that pierced the brick of the dome and travelled in the air, calling and calling hopelessly, hopefully, to the other side of the door.

FIVE

The cat still walks round the oak-tree, and it tells its story.

Now I have told you of the unfortunate, the lonely Safa Czarevich, I shall tell more of the old witch and her adopted daughter, the young witch Chingis – for, remember, Chingis is a witch now, and an apprentice no longer.

She had read and read in the big, heavy books kept in the old witch's oakwood chest: books written in shaman's alphabet and not easy to understand. But she had learned from them.

She had used the magic of words and music to change her shape, and the shape of other things; she had made trees walk in their bark. She had made herself so expert in questioning the shaman-drum that she never made a mistake, however complicated the message and faint the meaning. The old witch's pride in her could only be expressed by using the shaman's alphabet, which none of you could understand.

'Mothers and daughters are strangers to each other,' she told Chingis, 'but you are my witch-

61

daughter. You were my hard work, and are now my precious reward.'

A while after the old witch said, 'Chingis, I am near three hundred years old, and you need me no longer. I am tired of this old body, and I shall go into the ghost-world now, and grow another.'

'I shall visit you often,' said Chingis.

'You will always be welcome. I leave you my little house – never let its fire go out. I leave you my books – read them and learn. I leave you all my makers of music – play them often.'

'I promise I will, Grandmother.'

'And remember, it is your duty to write down all you learn, for our sisters and brothers in the future; and before you leave this world for the ghost-world, you must adopt a witch-daughter of your own, as I adopted you.'

'Send your spirit into a baby girl, Grandmother, and I will adopt you. What daughter could I love more than my own little grandmother?'

'That is the future; for now, help me to build my funeral pyre,' said the old witch.

They dragged logs from the clinging grip of grass and ferns, from the damp forest scents, and with these logs they built the base of the pyre. Armfuls of fallen branches, interwoven, raised it higher, and on that they piled layers of bark.

With many journeys and much patience, Chingis made a deep, soft bed of pine-needles on the top of the pyre, and she helped the old woman to climb it, and lie down.

From the hut Chingis brought a skin tent, a drum and a small harp, and placed them on the pyre beside the old witch. Food and drink she set near her too. And she bent over the old woman and kissed her before climbing down.

Chingis sat in the doorway of the house on chicken-legs and waited. For a long time the old woman was silent; then she took up the harp and, to a slow, darkening tune, she sang of every step a spirit must take on the way to the ghost-world. To Chingis the old woman's voice became fainter and thinner, as if it was reaching her over a longer and longer distance. And finally the voice called, from the very gate of the ghost-world. 'I have no more words in this world,' it said; and the voice and the music stopped.

The fire was slow to catch, but when it burned, it burned for three days, and the smoke rose straight into the sky without bending or drifting. A straight line of smoke between earth and sky – a sure sign that the spirit had made as straight and easy a journey.

The ashes of the pyre were of no importance, and Chingis went into the house on chicken-legs and rode away. So began her life alone, but she was never as alone as the Czarevich was. She read the books her witch-mother had left her, hearing the voices of the dead witches who had written them; and she practised her arts and slowly, sentence by sentence, wrote her own book. And she travelled, in her house on legs, and saw that for every stream there are a thousand streams, all the same and all different: that there are a thousand different trees, but that not even every birch-tree is the same as another; and that nothing in the world is content to be alone.

While the Czarevich, in the dark silence of his nut-like prison, searched inside his head for tawdry, weary trees of silk and sequins, and wooden animals all of the same shape, though painted different colours.

The pearl flowers, singing flames and truthful princesses of his imagination, which had once been so vivid and seemed so glorious to him, now seemed unutterably dreary. They had become grubby, thin and spoiled with over-use, as cloth does, however good the cloth was when first woven.

The weariness, the dreariness of the pictures in his head fed his longing to leave the dome-room. It was stronger than hunger, this longing, for it was never satisfied, or starved. It was stronger than iron, for it never rusted; stronger than bone, for it never broke; stronger than fire, for it never burned out. Every moment, day and night, waking and dreaming, his spirit cried; and circled and circled the dome-room, seeking a way out.

And Chingis heard.

She heard it first as she slept: a strange and eerily disturbing crying. Stepping from her body, her spirit grasped the thread of the cry and flew on it, like a kite on a line, to the Imperial Palace, to the highest tower, to the enamelled dome.

She flew about the dome, and heard the cry from within: she felt the cold and silence rising from the Palace. Then she turned away and stepped into another world.

But she remembered the cry and, when she awoke in this world, she listened for it. She listened beneath the nearby sounds of her house creaking, and the wind blowing; she heard the further sounds of the animals and birds in the forest around the house. Listening deeper, she heard the sounds of people talking in towns far away, and of the sea, still further away. Deeper than that, and she heard the sulky thoughts, the happy thoughts, the jumbled thoughts of a million people. Tilting and turning her head, at last she heard it – that eerie and endless moan, that cry from prison, that loneliness.

She took her drum and set it across her knees; placed the skull at its centre, and asked the question. 'Who is it that cries?'

She beat the drum, and the skittering, scratching, dragging skull slowly spelled out its answer. 'One who was born in a nutshell, and who is in danger.' That was the drum's answer in our alphabet. In the shaman's alphabet it told much more.

'What danger?' Chingis asked the drum.

'Death,' the drum spelled back: but with that one word it told her that the threat of death came from the Palace, that it came from those who should love the prisoner, and the future was not yet set and certain. Death might be turned aside.

Chingis laid aside her drum, and found a brush,

and ink made of soot. On a piece of birch-bark she painted a spell in the shaman's alphabet, and fastened the bark over the door of her house. The spell spelled out who was allowed to see the house on chicken-legs and who was not.

Chingis built up the fire in the stove until it was high and hot. The house began running on its chicken-legs, taking great strides and digging its claws deep. It ran over plains and through forests; it jumped rivers and passed by villages and towns, until it reached the Imperial City.

It strode through the gardens of the Palace, walked by guards, and folded its legs beneath it at the centre of an Imperial lawn. There it hunkered; a house, with a smoking stove-chimney and scaly chicken's-legs; and no one noticed it.

Chingis left the house and walked across the lawns towards the Palace. She was not seen because, as she went, she sang, and her song told all who heard it that she was not there. The gardeners, and the guards, heard a singing pass by them, but when they looked to see the singer, they saw only grass and flowers and sky.

Chingis followed a broad marble path, and climbed wide marble steps, to the massive bronze and gold doors of the Palace. As she climbed the steps she held both hands stretched before her – and the doors shuddered and clanged in their frame, and slowly moved inward, as if her hands were pressing a weight of air against them. 'But you shall see nothing, nothing that I do,' Chingis sang, and the guards on the steps and in the entrance hall did not see the doors opening, though they heard them open, and heard the singing. They heard the crash, too, and felt the floor shake, when Chingis dropped her hands to her sides and let both the bronze doors slam shut. The brazen noise reverberated far through the Palace, and every guard who heard it jumped and brought his pike into the fighting position. But there was no enemy to be seen, and the doors they heard slam had not, to their eyes, been opened. Only a singing passed through the hall and on into the jewel-coloured gloom of the Palace. The soldiers stood to attention, and feared ghosts.

In the corridors and on staircases Chingis passed servants and courtiers and more soldiers, who all seemed to dissolve and melt into frightened shadows of gold and red and deep blue-greens. They had heard a voice boldly and beautifully singing where even whispering was forbidden. People knelt as the voice approached them, crossed themselves, and ran from the haunted place when the voice had gone.

Patiently, Chingis made her way through the city of rooms and stairs. She had never been in such a place, but her life and training had prepared her for surprises. She reached the doorway of the highest tower.

The tower had a narrow entrance to its steep flight of steps. On either side stood guards. Singing, invisible, Chingis stepped between them.

She mounted the steps, spiralling round and round the tower's stones. With every few steps she passed a soldier, and every soldier she passed looked up, down, and all round at the sound of a softly singing woman's voice.

She reached the top of the tower and stood before the arched wooden door of the dome-room. The soldiers at the door looked across at each other with frightened faces.

Chingis stepped up to the door and laid her hand on it. The door leaped and rattled on its hinges, the lock revolved with a skreeking of metal. The soldiers jumped away from the door and stared – but though the door opened before their eyes and Chingis stepped through it, they only saw the closed, locked door they expected to see.

Inside the dome-room was dark, was thick air and a sour, musty smell. It was a sad, bad place.

Chingis stood still, and sang the song that birds sing at dawn. The song brought dawn into the room, brightening, until a clear, thin light lapped round the walls of the room as the light carried by water runs over the underside of a bridge.

Stone steps led from the door to the floor of the dome-room. Chingis climbed them and saw wreckage. From circling walls hung shreds of torn cloth. Tangles of sheet and coverings, cushions and stuffing and rags swamped the floor, hiding sharp splinters of broken wood and shards of dishes. Low tables were crowded to their edges with bowls of uneaten and mouldering food, the stink of it thickening the heavy and unmoving air. The bare walls were daubed and splattered with blackening, peeling food.

Chingis could not see the Czarevich but, as she waded through the mess of cloth and broken things, she stumbled and fell on to a low bed, half-submerged in the feathers, cushions, torn tapestries. On the bed, asleep, lay the Czarevich.

She moved the covers and cushions aside until she could see him clearly; and when she saw him, she thought him beautiful. 'Here is my apprentice,' she said.

She sat cross-legged on the bed, closed her eyes and stepped from her body into the Czarevich's dream. There all was dark and stinking, and the crying of the spirit that longed to leave that place was loud and disturbing. Chingis looked about her and saw a dozen ways out, but the Czarevich knew none of them. He knew only the dome-room.

In the dream Chingis opened the door of the room, and made windows. Light came in.

Safa Czarevich saw the light in his sleep, and, even in his dream, was astounded. He could not understand the light, and tried to make it firelight which he knew. Chingis would not allow it. In the dream the Czarevich moved his hands in daylight he had never seen awake. The light ran over his skin like water.

In the dream, by this new light, he saw a sharp-faced girl with black hair and black eyes. He knew her name, he knew she had come to help him, he

69

knew that he must and could trust her. He did not have to ask, or be told, any of this. That is how it is in dreams.

Chingis stood and held out her hand to him. He rose from his bed, put his hand into hers, and went with her. He neither knew nor wondered whether he was asleep or awake. In the dome-room there was little difference between sleeping and waking.

Down the steps they went to the door and, as they went down step by step, the door opened creak by creak, though no one had touched it. No soldiers came in.

Chingis was singing, and tugging on his hand.

They neared the door, and he could see through it – could see the soldiers, lit by the light that poured from the open door of the dome-room. Yet they seemed not to notice the light or the open door.

The door spread wider as they approached, gaping to let them through, to swallow them to the other side of the door.

Safa stopped, and pulled back towards the surety of his room. He remembered tigers. And he dreaded that, on the other side of the door, was another dome-room.

Chingis took both his hands and pulled him, with a snatch, with a snap, through to the other side.

They stood on a small, grey landing, crowded with two burly soldiers, who looked round, with scared faces, at the sound of the singing, but looked at the singer blindly.

Safa looked back and saw the door of his room

slam shut. He saw a strange blank wall with a blank, flat door set in it, closed. It was something he had never seen before.

He had never walked down such a long and winding flight of stairs before. He looked into the faces of innumerable soldiers, breathed in their faces, and they didn't see him. The stairs and the soldiers went on and on and if the stairs had gone on forever, if the world had proved to be nothing but an everlasting spiral stair, Safa would not have been disappointed or surprised. He didn't know what to expect of the other side of the door.

But the steps ended, and the floor was flat again, and there was no more circling round and round. They were in a corridor that stretched away in either direction. It was wonderfully lit with every dusky colour painted on its stone windows, but what was most wonderful, most wonderful, was that it was long, not round, and its walls and ceilings were flat! How was it not small and round? He would have stood and gaped, but Chingis tugged him on.

They passed a man who was not a soldier, who wore no greatcoat and carried no pike. The man didn't see them, but heard Chingis's singing and shrank away, and ran. Chingis wouldn't let Safa follow him, and she was right, for they passed many more people, both men and women. None of the women was Marien. All the people had different faces, though there were so many of them.

He had wished to see what lay on the other side of

the door, and now he knew. It was all walled and roofed. He had almost guessed that – but that there was so much of the world on the other side, he could never have guessed. Such long walks, such giant square rooms, rooms so huge that ten times five paces would not take you to the other side, corridors so long their other ends could not be seen. He was glad that Chingis held his hand and led the way. He felt so tiny, like a single stitch in the mass of embroidery covering his bedspread, like that single stitch undone.

And the colours! Before Marien had gone away there had been candlelight in the dome-room, showing him, in a dim and smoky way, the colours of cushions and toys – but there had never been these brilliant, gaudy, gorgeous colours that glowed in the windows as crowns and eagles and then, grown soft and feathery, blurred their rose, gold and blue over walls, ceilings and floors.

Now Chingis brought him down another staircase into the Palace entrance hall, and here Safa began to feel faint with the vastness of the world, for the entrance hall was neither square, nor oblong, nor round, but full of alcoves, niches and domes. It was higher and wider than all the other rooms he had seen. Chandeliers hung there; fountains spouted there, and living, scented flowering trees grew there. Safa clung to Chingis's hand, to make her stop. He wanted to know this place, this end of the world, and he needed to rest before his dizzy sight could begin to see it.

Chingis stretched out her hand and made the doors of the Palace open. The doors swung open, and Safa looked through them and saw that the Palace was not the whole world, as he had supposed. There was more.

Through the door – in a light that pained and needled his eyes – he saw green grass – white, blinding light – yellow flowers – scarlet uniforms.

Brighter, more brilliant, more fiery than flames were these colours. The grass was so hot a green that the red of his stove-fire would have paled beside it.

He covered his eyes with his hand. How can there be so much? He would not go towards the door.

Chingis pulled him forward, guided him through the door and down the marble steps. Safa felt the heat of a fire strike him and looked for the fire – but it was the fire in the distant sun he had felt.

He saw lawns and paths stretching so terrifyingly far that he felt his sight should not let him see so far. And then there were trees. And beyond the trees, church towers. And beyond the towers, and above his head, sky. The weight of the space and distance above and all about him pressed him down to his knees. Now he wished to go back to his dome-room, where there had been no light to scald his eyes, no such disturbing colours, and where a few steps had always brought him to a hard, comforting wall.

Chingis stood beside him, and into her song of invisibility, began to weave a call to her house. Across the lawns, on its chicken-legs, came the house, taking pompous, high-stepping strides. Its spell was still nailed over its door, and no one saw it come, except Chingis. Into her song she threaded a permission for Safa to see the house.

When the house was close, Chingis pulled him to his feet. He was not surprised to see a house on legs, and he looked back at the Palace to see what kind of legs *it* had. He could see none, and guessed that it was sitting on them, as the little house sat on its chicken-legs when it crouched to bring its door near the ground. Safa was glad to climb inside it, into a small, walled space again.

Chingis followed him inside. The doors closed, the house stood erect on its legs, and ran away from the Palace at a good speed.

So was Safa Czarevich brought out of imprisonment by the shaman, Chingis.

SIX

The learned cat still tramps about its tree, and there is still much of its gold chain to be wound up.

Chingis, the young witch, and Safa Czarevich, no longer lonely, have travelled away in the house on chicken-legs. Of them I shall tell no more for a while, but only for a while.

I shall tell instead (says the cat) of the Czar Guidon, and of the Imperial Princess Margaretta.

So the cat goes on walking, paw by paw, and the chain goes on winding, link by link.

The Strong and Compassionate, Ever-Ruling, Wise and Just Czar Guidon was sick, in a madness of fever, and not a doctor dared to treat him, for if the Czar died they might be blamed for his death. Round his bed the doctors stood, in twos and fours and sixes, and all of them swore together that nothing could be done, that indeed the best thing that could be done was nothing, and that the Czar's only hope for recovery was the prayers of his subjects. (The doctors, however, were praying that he would die and so never discover that they had refused to treat him.)

But the slaves who worked in the Palace gardens, rooms and kitchens prayed for the recovery of their Czar. They prayed because they were afraid that they might all be killed too, if the Czar died, so that he would not have to lie alone in his grave.

The Czar's courtiers also prayed that he would live, because if Czar Guidon died there would be a new Czar – or Czaritsa. The new Czar – or Czaritsa – might not like them. She – or he – might have them executed. Having Guidon as Czar was dangerous, but having Margaretta as Czaritsa would, for them, be worse.

'If Czar Guidon dies, then we must have Safa as Czar!' said the courtiers to each other. 'Czar Safa, long may he live, is the Czar for us! He is young and ignorant and has spent all his life in one room. Why, if you handed him a sharpened razor, he wouldn't know how to cut himself with it. If he was Czar, we could busy ourselves with cheating and stealing, and doing just as we please. Soon all of us would be rich! And when there were complaints, we could blame it all on our Glorious Czar Safa, and he wouldn't know how to begin calling us liars!'

'Brothers,' said the courtiers to each other, 'we must make sure that Safa, not Margaretta, is our next ruler.' And the courtiers began going secretly to the soldiers in the Palace, giving them money, and saying, 'Be ready, if Czar Guidon dies, to fight for us.'

The soldiers were happy, for a little while later along would come the Princess Margaretta, to give them more money, and rings and cap-brooches, saying, 'Take this and be ready, if Czar Guidon dies, to fight for *me*.' And then the Princess would go to her chapel, to pray that her brother would be taken to his well-deserved rest in Heaven. 'Let me ascend to the Czar-chair, dear God,' prayed Margaretta, 'and I will serve Thee truly and faithfully, and all Thy commandments shall be kept in my Czardom.'

God helps those who help themselves, so Margaretta did not sit in her room eating sweets and waiting for God to bring all to pass. She went about the Palace, saying to the soldiers she had bought, 'When the death-bell rings for Czar Guidon, run, run and arrest the courtiers. Arrest them all and hold them prisoner until I am Czaritsa and give you further orders.' To other soldiers, those whom she was most certain she had fooled with her promises, she gave more precious gifts and said, 'The moment the old Czar dies, run, run to the tower-room, to my nephew, Safa. Take the pillows from his bed and smother him. Tell no one I told you to do it, and when I am Czaritsa, I shall make you all generals.'

They were fools to believe her, because she intended to give them, once they had carried out her orders, a grave each. But no matter how many lies Czars and Czaritsas tell, they always seem to find enough fools to believe the next lie.

Often, when she was on her way through the stained-glass twilight of the Palace to speak to her soldiers, the Princess would pass a courtier who was on his way to speak to the soldiers he had bought for the courtiers' side. And the courtiers whispered into the ears of the soldiers, 'When you hear the bell ring for the Czar Guidon's death, run, run to the tower-room and stand guard over the Czarevich Safa, and protect him from his enemies. You will all be made lords when he is made Czar.'

To other soldiers, the courtiers said, 'The moment you know the old Czar is dead, run, run to the apartments of the Princess Margaretta. Chop her down, kill her. Be very sure you don't leave her alive, and you will be rewarded.'

Czar Guidon died in the middle of the night, much to the relief of his doctors. A doctor opened the door to the Czar's room and spoke to the two guards outside, asking them to give the order for the Czar's death-bell to be rung.

Now one of these guards was in the pay of the courtiers, and the other was in the pay of Princess Margaretta. Both guards set off running – but not to ring the bell.

Through all the long years of the Czar Guidon's reign, a deep silence had been kept in all the miles of passages. The silence was shattered at last, not by the awful ringing of the death-bell, but by excited, ringing shouts, by the fast sound of booted, running feet, by the rattle and hiss of drum-beats, by screams and cries of pain and fear, by laughter, the crash of things thrown down, of doors slammed and doors broken. The silence, that had been so carefully stored for so many years in those rooms and corridors, vanished in a second.

In the passages and rooms of the Princess Margaretta's apartments, a fierce battle was being fought between those soldiers hired by the Princess and those hired by the courtiers. The court-rooms were filling with soldiers battling to defend the courtiers or arrest them.

The narrow stairs of the tower leading to the dome-room were made horrible with the most desperate battle of all – a three-sided battle between Safa's Guard, defending the stairs; Margaretta's Own, who wished to fight their way up the stairs and smother the Czarevich; and the courtiers' soldiers, who wished to take the Czarevich prisoner.

In the midst of the uproar, the panic, the killing, the heavy bell of the chapel began tolling, rolling its weighty noise over the shriller screams and cries of the fighting, announcing the death of Czar Guidon. All the churches of the Imperial City began ringing their bells; and then the churches further away set their bells swinging, until every church in the Czardom was ringing its bells to mark the death of the Czar, though the bells told nothing of the battle being fought in the Palace, and the many deaths in its corridors.

The battle on the steps of the tower was the first to end, though it had been the fiercest. There was so little room that a blow aimed at one man would be knocked aside to injure another. No matter how hard they struggled, or how bravely they pushed forward, the attacking soldiers were always driven back down the stairs into the passage. Dead soldiers were thrown down after them, and made a barricade with their bodies.

All were exhausted, and the fighting stopped. Margaretta's soldiers drew together at one side of the stairs, and the courtiers' soldiers to the other. Safa's Guards blocked the steps.

Sweating, lank-haired, breathless and blood-stained, the soldiers eyed each other. None of them wanted to start fighting again, but they all had their futures to think of.

Out from the courtiers' soldiers stepped a young man, named Vanya. He laid down his sword and held up his hands, to show he meant no one any harm.

'Brothers,' he shouted, in the sound of the bell, 'why are we killing each other? None of us should have been hurt. It's only this Czarevich that needs to be hurt.'

All the soldiers, even those on the stairs, listened.

'Myself, I don't wish the Czarevich any harm either,' Vanya yelled. 'Nor do my brothers in the courtiers' pay, nor do my brothers on the stairs here. It's only you, brothers, fighting for Margaretta, who wish to hurt him.'

'We don't either,' one of Margaretta's soldiers shouted back. 'We only want to smother him.'

'But suppose you win this fight, and you smother him,' said Vanya. 'And then suppose that our brothers elsewhere in the Palace have chopped the

80

Princess to bits. What will you do then, brothers?'

The soldiers on the stairs and in the courtiers' company laughed, while Margaretta's Own stood red-faced, baffled and angry.

'We should have a Czar-chair and neither Czar nor Czaritsa to sit on it,' shouted Vanya. 'The courtiers would have to fight each other to decide which one of them will be the next Czar. And *you* would all be executed, brothers.'

Now Margaretta's soldiers looked afraid, but Vanya turned sharply to the laughing soldiers of Safa's Guard on the stairs.

'And you, brothers! You are carrying out the orders of a dead man. Don't you hear the bell? Do you think we would be fighting if Guidon still ruled? Maybe the courtiers will win, maybe Margaretta will, but one thing is certain, brothers – your Czar Guidon won't.'

Safa's Guard all looked so crestfallen that the soldiers in the corridor laughed aloud.

'Look at the dead men here. Our brothers – born in the same land, raised in the same poverty – not sons of the same parents, but sons of the same slavery, brothers! And we killed them to please rich courtiers, to please an Imperial Princess, to please a dead Czar! What are we doing, brothers, to kill each other for these rich strangers, who own us and work us like animals?'

Now all the soldiers, no matter whose side they were on, nodded and agreed. 'What shall we do then, Vanya?' one of them called; and from the stairs, from all sides, came the cry, 'Tell us what to do then, little brother.'

'We must join together and not fight each other,' Vanya shouted. 'What is it to us who sits on the Czar-chair? Whoever it is will treat us as slaves just as Guidon did; whoever it is will need soldiers. I'll tell you what we will do, brothers: we will all go up the stairs and take the Czarevich prisoner. Then we will play cards and tell stories until we find out who has won. If the courtiers win, we'll hand the Czarevich over to them safe and sound, and we'll be rewarded. If Margaretta wins, well then, we'll smother the lad and present her with his body, and she'll reward us. So, brothers!'

One of the soldiers on the stairs, an old man with long grey moustaches and a long grey beard, shouted out, 'The Czarevich is a boy, and he's mad. It would be a shame to take him prisoner and then to smother him.'

'A shame, a shame,' Vanya yelled. 'Many things are a shame. Three of my brothers and two of my sisters died of cold and hunger – that was a great shame, but I don't remember the Czarevich, or his auntie, or his dad being too tearful about it. Anyway, Grandfather, the courtiers might win – or, if they don't, you can leave us to do the smothering while you go off and pretend that no prince was ever murdered on his relative's orders.'

None of the other soldiers objected. They were shaking hands, and hugging and kissing; and all together they climbed the narrow tower to the dome-room at the top. The chapel bell still rang for Guidon's death, and the stones of the tower shook beneath their feet.

The soldiers jammed the landing and stairs while the door of the dome-room was unlocked. Then they all crowded forward, shouting for candles and lanterns, which were passed in over their heads. It didn't take many of them to fill the dome-room. Not one of them could see the Czarevich anywhere.

All the wreckage in the room – the torn tapestries and sheets – the ripped cushions and splintered furniture – the smashed toys and dishes, the uneaten food – all this was thrown from the room and kicked down the stairs. The room was stripped to the bare wooden floor and its bare brick wall. The Czarevich could not be found. He was not there.

Now the soldiers began to take sides again. The courtiers' soldiers and Margaretta's Own drew together and said to the men of Safa's Guard, 'You helped his escape. You felt sorry for him and let him go. You should not have done it, brothers, because now you've made danger for us all. What will happen when we have to say that we have neither the Czarevich nor his dead body?'

Safa's Guard shouted back that none of them had helped in any escape. They had kept the door locked and guarded it. No one had come in or gone out . . . But there had been a mysterious singing heard . . . Yes, and the door had *sounded* as if it had opened, though it had remained closed. 'It was a miracle,' shouted the old soldier. 'The Virgin and the saints came and carried him away.'

'Perhaps the saints will do us a good turn, and carry us away when Margaretta wants to know what's happened to her nephew!' yelled another.

'What shall we do?' they all asked, and the questions gabbled in the curve of the dome. No one will believe us, they said. We'll be tortured and executed for helping him to escape, and we didn't! We did our duty, and our houses will be burned as a punishment for not carrying out orders. What shall we do? Vanya, what shall we do? Shall we tell the truth? The truth always saves an honest man. Vanya, is that a good idea?

'The man who tells the truth must be mounted on a fast horse,' Vanya shouted. 'Brothers, we are worrying far too soon. One of us must go and find out who has won, if anyone has yet – the courtiers or Margaretta. Once we know that, we shall know better what to do. And I volunteer to go myself and find out.'

The others applauded, kissed him, hugged him, shook his hands; and they sent him off down the stone stairs while they settled themselves to gambling and gossip and long stories.

Vanya ran down the stairs and jumped the pile of dead bodies at the bottom. The deep, crashing, shuddering bell was still ringing for the death of the Czar, and nothing else could be heard. The noise of the bell so filled the Palace that it was almost as if it was silent again. Vanya met no one as he made his way through the complicated corridors. The servants were hiding.

84

In the apartments of the Imperial Princess there was the noise of the bell, and destruction. Sword-slashes marked the wooden panelling of the walls and had left the hangings in rags; blood stained the carpets, cushions and chairs. The rooms smelt of blood. Dead soldiers lay underfoot still, but there was no Princess, living or dead.

Vanya left the place, and made his way, through the noise of the bell, to the court-rooms. When he was at the door he could hear other sounds, under the din of the bell – there were voices singing and shouting, and drums beating. He went into the court-room and saw, at the foot of the Czar-chair's steps, a heap of courtiers, all tied together in a bundle. All round them, soldiers were celebrating.

'Vanya, our Vanya!' said these soldiers, and pulled Vanya in, kissed him and poured him drink. 'Drink to our Czaritsa!' they said. 'We are all her soldiers now, and we shall have a palaceful of new courtiers!'

Vanya drank health and long life to the Czaritsa Margaretta, and asked where she might be. No one knew, but she hadn't been killed, and her soldiers had won. Long live Margaretta! A long reign to Margaretta!

Vanya left as soon as he could, and hurried back to the dome-room at the top of the tower. The great bell still rang. No wonder they ring such a loud bell for the death of Czars, he thought: it must ring for the deaths of many others too.

He had to gasp for breath when he reached the

dome; and all the soldiers left off their stories and their card-games to sit up and listen to him. The first words he spoke were, 'Long live the Czaritsa Margaretta!' and then they knew who had won and groaned aloud.

'Brothers,' said Vanya, dropping down among them, and cupping his hands about his mouth to yell, 'Margaretta will want to see the Czarevich's body so she can be sure he's dead. Brothers, we have no choice. We must go to the forests and be bandits.'

At once there was disagreement. Cards and caps were flung down and booted feet stamped.

'Grub in a forest like pigs! Live that miserable existence!'

'What of us, who are old? Forests are cold and wet.'

'They are worse than cold and wet in winter.'

'Brothers, I know the life of a bandit is miserable,' Vanya said, 'but it is a life. I think we should leave at once while we still have unbroken legs to run on.'

They began to argue again, but Vanya got to his feet and shouted, 'Brothers, brothers – we are all soldiers of the Czar, so we know all about being cold and hungry and living a hard life. Why are we whining about a little snow and rain? We are all slaves: that means we could make a life on a small rock in a wide sea if we helped each other. What are we afraid of? Let those who have wives and children run and fetch them, or tell them to follow after, and the rest of you, come with me.'

Almost all of the soldiers rose and followed Vanya. They ran through the Palace kitchens, cramming food into sacks. In the stables and yards they helped themselves to fuel, axes and horses. They ran home to their huts and families.

In less than two hours Vanya's company, with horses, children, wives, and even old parents who could not be left behind, were on their way into the forest, there to live as outlaws, as runaway slaves, and as bandits. Their journey takes them right out of this story for a while, but not for ever.

Of all Vanya's company only three men, three very old men who could not face life in the forest, stayed behind. 'What of the winter?' they said to each other. 'We're more likely to get mercy from the Czaritsa Margaretta than from Old January in the forest.' And these three old soldiers marched off to join the party in the court-room, and very drunk they got there.

Where had the Imperial Princess Margaretta hidden herself to escape murder? No one knew, which is why she was not found; and the day after her brother's death she walked into the court-room, climbed the flight of steps to the peacock-backed Czar-chair, and seated herself on it. As she sat, the rolling, dull, deafening noise of the death-bell stopped. The soldiers gathered about the steps and cheered for the new Czaritsa.

'I am pleased that you love me, my children,' Margaretta said to them, 'but from this day forward, the rule of silence will be observed. God has given me the victory; I am God on earth in female form. My Godhead must not be offended by vulgar noise.'

A deep silence fell, spreading out through the Palace.

'The first act of my reign must be to clear away the rubbish of my brother's.' Margaretta pointed to the heap of bound courtiers. 'The day is before you, my children,' she said to the soldiers. 'Take them and kill them, and bury them out of sight before the sun sets.'

She watched as a troop of soldiers was detailed, and they dragged and bullied the courtiers from the room. Those remaining, soldiers and nobles, were silent, very silent, as the fear of death touched them all. Margaretta looked down on them from the Czar-chair and patted the arm of that magnificent chair with satisfaction.

'I shall replace my ministers when I have had time to consider who shall most please me and most faithfully obey me,' she said. 'But now we have a happier matter to deal with. I wish my poor nephew to be released from his long imprisonment. I sent men to release him. Where are they? Where is he?'

Czaritsa Margaretta waited, with a motherly smile, for someone to step forward and answer her questions. No one did. The three old men who had deserted from Vanya's company began to shake.

'What? Did I not give orders? Where is my nephew?' the Czaritsa demanded.

Everyone looked at the floor and said nothing.

'Bring my nephew before me now!' cried the

Czaritsa, and banged the arm of the Czar-chair.

The three old soldiers whispered in each other's ears, and then slowly went forward to the steps of the Czar-chair. They knelt awkwardly and bowed their faces to the floor, and the bravest of the three cried out, 'Do not punish us, Mighty Czaritsa, but give us permission to speak.'

Margaretta waved her hand, and a captain yelled, 'Speak!'

'Mighty and merciful Czaritsa,' said the old soldier, 'we were among those ordered to smother the –'

'Ordered to *what*?' the Czaritsa snapped.

The soldier was old and his mind muddled. 'Ordered to – ordered to murder the Czarevich, Czaritsa, to smother – '

Margaretta leaned forward in her chair. 'Who gave you orders to murder my nephew? *I* gave no such orders. Tell me who ordered you to do this, and I will have them executed.'

Nothing bewilders a simple man like a deliberate lie which everyone knows to be a lie. The old soldier stammered and muttered to himself. The second old soldier hastily spoke up.

'We went to release the lad, Czaritsa – but we could find no trace of him, alive or dead. The dome-room was locked – but when we unlocked it, it was empty, Czaritsa.'

The Czaritsa was frozen in her chair. Those who dared to look up at her saw her face turn white. 'Those three,' she said, pointing to the three old

89

soldiers, 'they know what has happened to my nephew. He has been kidnapped, and they know where he has been taken. Take them and torture them – let us have the truth from them. I must have my nephew restored to me.'

The Czaritsa then went to the new apartments she had chosen for herself, where the walls were panelled in sheets of amber. The three old soldiers were taken to much larger apartments, the Imperial Torture Chambers, where they told all sorts of stories besides the truth; and remarked several times that they wished they had gone to spend January in the forest. But nothing they said was believed.

All that the three soldiers said was written down and taken to the Czaritsa in her amber-walled apartments. Squads of soldiers searched the Palace and countryside, and threatened and questioned the people, in a search for any sign or news there might be of Safa Czarevich. There were no signs and no news. Sometimes the Czaritsa would find herself believing that there never had been a Czarevich. She had never seen him. Perhaps the dome-room had always been empty. But in the night she would wake in a horror of cold from a dream of that Czarevich taking the crown from her head and throwing her down the steps of the Czar-chair. Whatever she pretended, she wanted to see the Czarevich's dead body and know for certain that he was dead.

The Czaritsa had a proclamation made throughout

the Czardom. The Czaritsa feared and grieved for her beloved nephew, the proclamation said. She feared that wicked people who hated God and freedom and peace had kidnapped the poor boy and were going to try and make him Czar in place of her, the Holy Czaritsa, appointed by God. Then the whole unhappy Czardom would be plunged into a dreadful war. Thousands would be killed; thousands would be driven from their homes; thousands would die from hunger and cold. She begged her loyal people to do all they could to deliver the poor, simple-minded Czarevich into her loving hands. Then there would be no war and no suffering.

A million people throughout the Czardom heard it. Not one of them believed it. 'Who doesn't know where the young prince is?' they asked one another. 'Everyone knows he's in the grave they dug for him after our Holy Czaritsa had him murdered.'

And, but for the witch Chingis, they would have been right.

SEVEN

Round the tree goes the cat on the golden chain, telling its story.

Of course Safa Czarevich is not in a grave, says the cat. He has been taken as an apprentice by the witch, Chingis: and it is of them that I shall tell now.

To Safa, the variety and beauty of the world was shocking; and the shock never ended.

He had spent his life in a dark, small room in a silent palace. Five steps had always brought him against a wall. Now space glowed and spread about and above him, offering distances that could never be paced out. He felt the dust-motes at his finger-tips tingle in companionship with dust-motes that flew – how far? – above his head, buzzing in clouds. The recklessness of the unwalled space about him dizzied him each time he lifted his head.

He had thought Marien unendingly different and absorbing in her moods and expressions. Add Chingis, and all her moods, all her knowledge, all her changeability – and surely that was enough? But no: there were scores of women, more than could be counted or remembered, and they all had different faces, different voices, changing moods, changing thoughts. How could so much difference be?

Not all men were soldiers, or even Palace servants. Not all people were men or women. Some were children, boys and girls, the same, and yet different from the larger animal, and all different from one another. He could not bear to think of it all for long at a time. It exhausted him.

He had been told of forests by Marien, and had imagined them as forests of twining embroidery and glittering sequins. To the eyes of someone bored with real, dusty, dirty, living forests, these frail growths of silk and tinsel might seem pretty and charming – but to Safa the weight, the mass, the smell, the living, upward growth of the real trees overwhelmed all thought and filled him with delight. All the different trees, covering the land for such grand, unknowable distances, heaping the ground with centuries of fallen leaves and branches. The real, the ordinary, outdid all imagination.

Not one kind of flower, but many, many flowers; nor one kind of fish nor one kind of bird – and a fish and bird so wonderfully different that a fish was never mistaken for a bird nor a bird for a fish, though some fish flew and some birds swam! Difference, difference in everything. The light changed from morning, to afternoon, to evening; and even from minute to minute as clouds passed over the sun. The darkness of the open air was different from the darkness he had lived his life in, and it was a darkness that changed as often as light.

The air changed its touch against his face, the scents it carried to his nose, the sounds it brought to his ear. The sound of an axe was different if heard at evening or mid-day; and different if it was distant or close by.

He was a poor apprentice. He was so mad with the variety of things that he could be taught nothing. If the spirit that lived in his head had once called and called for release from the dome, now it babbled to itself in a never-ending song of exclamation. Chingis heard the song always, and learned new music from it – and learned to see anew things which even a witch comes to think of as ordinary.

But listen, (says the cat) and I'll tell you of Kuzma.

Do you remember the shaman, Kuzma, who lived far to the north, and harvested the ice-apples?

He was jealous and fearful of Chingis, because she was so clever a witch, and he often watched her in his shaman's mirror. He hated to see her reading or writing, because he knew she was adding to her knowledge and power, and he feared that she was becoming so great a witch that he could never hope to better her.

He was furious and fearful when he saw that Chingis had done what she was not meant to do, and had taken an apprentice, though she was still so young herself. And had taken a male apprentice! And one who was not new-born!

He could not understand why Chingis had done this, and was angry that she dared to break the custom of witches, but fearful that she might succeed in some way that no other witch before her ever had.

He rejoiced when he saw that the boy was unteachable, and could not learn even the simplest word-magic. But he was suspicious when he saw that Chingis was not angry, and wrote more and more in her book.

Kuzma watched in his mirror until Chingis slept, and he sent his spirit to her hut, where it stood beside her table and blew over the pages of her book. There it read of how much she had learned from her unteachable apprentice; and it read of much it didn't understand. Shivering with apprehension, it whisked back to its body.

The summer passed. Now the days were short, and cold, and growing colder. Frost came, hardened the ground and traced it with white. Ice began to snap in the tree-tops and to squeeze even Chingis's house. It grew colder still, and then the snow came. Flakes of snow fell and fell until they lay so deep that Safa stood knee-deep in them. How could there be so many of the tiny snowflakes that they could lie so deep over the whole world?

The sap froze in trees. Bears had long since gone to sleep, and the geese flown away. And people were hungry. Do you remember the soldiers who ran from the Imperial Palace rather than face the Czaritsa with the news that her nephew had escaped them? Listen (says the cat) and I'll tell of them.

Those soldiers had come, with their families, to

the forest, and they had suffered a hard, bad time of it. They were still alive, but they didn't expect to be for much longer. Rightly fearing the winter, they had put the best of their labour into building houses, three big houses, to shelter all their people from the cold weather. But the work had taken so long that they had not had the time, or the people, to collect enough food to feed them through the cold, dark months. Nor did the stoves in the houses keep them as warm as stoves should, because stove-setting is a skilled trade, not to be undertaken by just anyone. So winter had come too soon for them, and they were starving.

The men and women went out to hunt and snare and grub for what they could, but such work, in deep snow, is cold, hungry and exhausting. Besides, the hunter is not lucky every day. The people grew thinner and weaker, and were not able to work as long. So they came to famine. The three long-houses of their village were dark; and the people lay in them, measuring their remaining time in their own slow heart-beats, and mouthfuls of food.

But though their bodies were weak, and growing weaker, the spirits that lived in many of them were alive, and strong, and furious. They didn't want to lose their bodies; they were afraid. They cried out, continuously, angry and screeching at their coming death. And other spirits, who were old and tired, still kept up a sad and constant weeping beneath the noise of their stronger fellows.

Every witch in the Czardom heard the part-song

of this spirit choir; they could not fail to hear it. But not every witch was inclined to listen.

Chingis heard, and Chingis listened.

She said to Safa, 'Little brother; do you remember that place where you used to live? Do you remember the soldiers who stood on the other side of the door?'

'I remember,' he said.

She caught his hand and said, 'Listen!'

He listened hard, and thought that he caught a sound, unlike the sounds he had learned to know. It was a sound so faint that it was no sound, and yet it made him afraid, and he pulled his hand away from Chingis.

'That's the crying of spirits who know they must die,' Chingis said. 'A witch hears it always – but I am the cause of these deaths. Nothing can be altered without altering everything that touches it. When I took you from your prison, Safa, I drove those poor souls towards their deaths. I think I must help them too.'

'Yes – help them,' Safa said. He had a vague notion that the souls she spoke of were imprisoned in a dark, close place, and were crying to be released. 'Bring them out – let them live with us.'

Chingis roused from her thinking and laughed at him. 'They wouldn't want to live with us, little brother; but yes! We shall help them. Bring me my drum – and a bowl of salt – and we shall find food for them.'

Safa ran after the hut – which had wandered

away, scratching the ground, on its chicken-legs – and fetched from it Chingis's large, flat drum, and a bowl of ground salt from the cupboard. He brought them to Chingis, and she took the salt and, with it, made a wide circle in the snow. The salt melted a deep groove to mark the circle, and they were inside it. Then Chingis sat cross-legged in the snow and set the drum across her knees. Safa knelt beside her. 'Stay within the circle,' she said to him. 'Whatever you see and whatever you hear, do not speak; and stay in the circle.'

Safa nodded. He had learned that what Chingis said, she meant; and what she meant, she said. So he would not speak or move, but became all intent on seeing and hearing whatever it might be that she would call to the circle.

Chingis began to drum. It was not the steady, monotonous drumming she used for questioning, but a rhythmic, insistent drumming that jerked itself away from its own pattern each time he thought he had learned it. Chingis threw up her voice and sent it weaving, rising and falling, through the sound of the drumming. She was calling to something, and Safa twisted his head round, looking into the winter darkness and forest shadows, to see what would answer her call. The touch of the air and darkness on his skin changed, cooled, and something came nearer. He pressed closer to Chingis, though he was well within the circle.

Shapes came gathering to the edges of the circle,

shapes that drifted and brought with them the shining darkness of a night when snow falls thickly. A long, ribboning wolf-shape wound round and round the circle restlessly, and Safa smelt a stink of wolf and felt a cold, cold air touch his face. A bear-shape, high and huge, came prowling, and as its heavy fur rippled there was a glittering, as if snow-stars were trapped in its thickness. There came the shifting, melting shapes of birds and deer. Even fish-shapes came swimming through the air, their flanks glinting with snow-scales.

Chingis began to speak to these spirits, using a language which Safa understood only when he did not try to understand it, and not always then. But she told the spirits of the other spirits nearby who were crying out in terror because their bodies were dying. 'Tell me of your sisters who are trapped in old and painful bodies,' she said to the spirits. 'If they will give their bodies to these starving people, I will give them an easy death. I will lead them to the ghost-world; death need have no fear for them.'

Safa heard, faintly, the sounds of animals, the growling, the coughing and snuffling. Yet the animal spirits were close around him. The bear-spirit raised itself and hung over them, stars of ice — or stars, perhaps — rippling in its fur. It spoke to Chingis in a voice so deep and distant Safa could hardly hear it, and in a language he could not understand. Chingis answered, and the bear spoke again. It seemed to Safa that they spoke sleepily, and he felt sleepy from the cold that surrounded the salt circle, a dry and stifling cold. He rested his head on Chingis's shoulder and was closing his eyes when she struck the drum with loud, sharp blows, like the sudden and unreal noise that wakes you from a dream. His head jerked up from Chingis's shoulder, and he caught so fleeting a glimpse of the animals drifting into the darkness that he might not have seen them at all.

The hut on chicken-legs was not far away, crouching with its door close to the ground. Chingis led the way to it, and they warmed themselves on its stove.

'I must leave you for a little while,' Chingis said. 'I must find an old bear with a broken jaw. I must ease her pain and fear, and lead her to the ghost-world. No!' she said, when she saw that Safa would ask to go with her. 'You may not come near the ghost-world. But I will leave you with a job to do for me. Stay here with my house, and keep its fire alight – never let my house starve or I shall make you sorry! Wait here until a white bird comes and perches on the roof and calls you. It will be a white bird, white all over, and it will call your name. Follow it, and it will lead you to the soldiers who used to guard your room, to them and to their families. Fetch them from their houses, tell them you have food for them. Follow the bird again, and it will lead you to me, and to the bear. Now, repeat what you have to do.'

Safa repeated it all, and Chingis kissed him, took her drum, and left him.

For two long, dark days Safa was alone in the hut.

He kept the fire alight, and amused himself by examining the drums and flutes hung on the walls, and by turning the pages of the books he could not read. He found, at the bottom of a chest, a long shaman's robe, like the one Chingis wore, and a tall, embroidered shaman's hat, and he put them both on. He ate when he was hungry, and told himself stories and sang himself songs. And then he heard his name being sung in the dark outside. 'Safa! Safa!'

He went out into the snow and saw, perched on the carved edge of the wooden roof, a bird so white it shone dimly in the darkness. And it sang, 'Safa! Safa!'

'I hear you,' he said to it, and it flew from the roof and away into the trees. Safa followed, dragging his feet through the heavy snow, often stumbling, often losing himself in the darkness. But then the bird would call out his name from a nearby tree, and he would find it again. And so the bird led him to the village in the forest, to the three long-houses where the soldiers and their families were starving. The bird flew to the roof of the first house, just above its door, and perched there. Safa leaned on the wooden door and pushed, and walked in.

It was so dark inside the house that the fire shining from the open door of the stove could only smear a dim sheen of light over the darkness. The people sitting and lying wearily in that darkness heard the outer door of their home open and close, and wondered dully who could be coming in. Some thought they had dreamed the sound. But the inner door opened, and an upright figure came in among them.

Still some thought they dreamed. In the dim light beads, coins and shells glimmered over the long robe the stranger wore. A woman near the stove poked a stick in the fire until the end flamed, and then held it up as a torch. By its leaping, flaming light they saw their visitor fully for a second, and then not at all – and then the figure would be lit by another flare. What they saw in this flickering way, frightened them.

They saw a figure dressed in the long, beaded, tasselled robe of a witch, with an outlandish hat on its head, and thick mittens and soft, thick-soled boots, all covered in Lappish embroidery. They recognized the clothes of a northern witch.

And then, worse, for an old soldier suddenly snatched the torch, and held it closer to the visitor. This old soldier had guarded the dome-room for many years, and now he said, 'That is the face of Safa Czarevich!'

And others looked, and recognized the face too. 'A ghost,' they said.

'Why have you come here?' shouted the old soldier with the torch.

'I have come to fetch you,' said Safa.

A moan of sheer terror rose from the people. This ghost, this Lappish witch, had come in from the winter darkness to fetch away their souls.

'There is food for you close by here,' Safa said.

'Come with me, and the bird will lead us to it.'

At the promise of food, people struggled to rise, and were dragged down again by others. There was a bubbling moan of fear and hope. How can you trust such a creature, that has taken another's face, people were asking. Others said, 'Never trust and never gain.'

Safa could not understand why they didn't follow him at once, and stood bewildered while they argued over whether they should try to kill him or drive him away; or if they should beg his mercy and pray to him.

Then it was suggested that Vanya should be sent for; and to that everyone agreed. Vanya had led them from the Palace and got them into this danger; let Vanya decide what should be done. A boy was sent to fetch Vanya from another of the long-houses as quickly as possible.

Vanya was told the Czarevich's ghost had come to trouble them, and he floundered through the snow to the house, and stood close to the strange vistor, staring. Vanya's starved face was full of shadowed hollows and sharp, shining ridges of bone. 'Have you come to haunt us?' Vanya asked. 'We didn't kill you. Don't blame us for your death.'

'You need food,' Safa said. 'Come with me, and I'll take you to where there is food for you.'

'What shall we do, Vanya?' the people asked. 'Is it a trick? Shall we kill him? *Can* we kill him?'

'You say you'll take us to food,' Vanya said. 'Why do you want to help us?'

'Because I was in the dome,' Safa said.

'It *is* the Czarevich!' everyone said. 'Did you hear him?'

'Perhaps he has come to help us,' they whispered. 'The dead have been known to return to help the living.'

'Remember, his mother was a slave, like us, before they made her a Czaritsa – and how like her he is!'

'Look at his face,' came other whispers. 'There's nothing wicked there. This isn't an evil ghost.'

'But why is he dressed like a witch?' was asked; and no one could answer it. And all fell silent. They waited for Vanya to decide what was to be done.

Safa took Vanya's hand in his own mittened one and said, 'If you will come with me, I will take you to a bear that you can eat.'

Vanya decided to trust him, and said, 'Everyone who has good clothes against the cold, and a weapon, come with us. Go on, your Imperial Ghostliness.'

So the strongest of those left gathered together their warmest clothes, and whatever weapons they had, and followed Safa from the house. A white bird flew from the roof of the house and, as it flew, it called, 'Safa, Safa, Safa!' Safa followed the bird as it flew ahead of them into the trees, and the people of the village followed Safa. They were more than ever convinced that what led them was a ghost or a witch's devil. A white bird, with not a speck of colour on it anywhere, a bird such as none of them had ever seen – a bird that waited for them, and called them to follow it by crying out a name in human speech! If they had not so desperately needed food, they would have run away.

The bird and Safa led them a long way through the snow and the people, already weak from hunger and cold, were stumbling and falling from sheer exhaustion when the bird suddenly dipped from the air and perched on something large and dark that lay in the snow. It was the body of a bear, just as the witch-boy had promised them.

Several of the people lifted their tired feet and made a dash for the bear, but then stopped suddenly, with spurts of snow from their boot-heels. They had seen the white bird rise from the bear's corpse and fly away. They followed its flight and saw it light on the shoulder of a woman who stood at a little distance from the bear. She was hard to see in the winter dark, but they could see she wore a tall cap, and a long, tasselled robe; and they recognized the shape of the large, round, flat drum slung at her back. This was a witch: the owner of the devil who had lured them to her. And there, still further away and crouching among the trees, was the witch's hut, crouching on its chicken-legs, a light shining in its window. The villagers pressed together in a tight little group, and held each others' hands and arms.

The witch raised her hand and beckoned her devil to her side. She whispered to him while the villagers watched fearfully.

The devil with the Czarevich's face turned to the people and shouted, 'Chingis says, take the bear and eat it, and do not fear that its spirit will haunt you. It was old, sick, and glad to die. She says, do not be afraid of the future; she will see you safely through the winter.'

Hand in hand, the witch and her devil walked away through the darkness to their hut. The devil often looked back and smiled and waved; but the witch never looked back.

Vanya and his companions watched them enter the hut; and they watched the hut rise on its giant, scaly chicken-legs, and walk away. The finicky manner in which the giant legs picked and scratched, with the little hut perched on top of them, was comic, but no one laughed. Many things which are funny to imagine are humourless when they happen before your eyes.

Long after the hut and the glimmer of light from its window had disappeared, the villagers still stood huddled together, not daring to approach where a witch had been. Vanya saw that it was up to him, and he said, 'Come! We can't stand here till we freeze into one block! Let's joint that bear and get it back to our cooking pots as fast as we can!'

But still no one moved.

'Brothers! Sisters!' Vanya said. 'If the witch had meant us harm, we'd be changed into bears ourselves by now. But look at me! Do I look like a bear?'

'No more than usual, Vanya,' they said, and laughed. The skin of their lips split in the cold. But they all hurried to the bear and began to chop it into joints with axes and knives, and then to drag and carry it home across the snow.

Many hungry hours went by before they had the bear back at the village, and cooked, but then everyone ate as much as they could, and some made themselves ill.

And after that, throughout the winter, whenever the village's stocks of food and hope were failing, the doors of one or another of the houses would open, and in would come the witch's devil with the Czarevich's face; and he, and the white bird, would lead the way to the tough and scrawny carcass of some old creature – a deer, a bear, a wolf, a fox.

It made the villagers feel special and protected to be helped in this way by a witch and a devil, but it was alarming too. *Why* was the witch feeding them?

'Ah, that's easy. She's fattening us up for her own cooking pot!'

'Well, I don't see any of us growing fat,' Vanya said. 'So, if we are to be boiled, it won't be for a long time – eat and forget about it!'

And that is all I have to say about the people, the witches and the devils in the forest for a while.

EIGHT

The cat is still circling the oak-tree, telling its tale.

Do you remember the shaman Kuzma, who looked in his brass mirror and saw a greater shaman than he?

And do you remember the new Czaritsa, the Czaritsa Margaretta, who longs to embrace her nephew again, the easier to stab him in the back?

I shall begin (says the cat) by telling of her.

None of the proclamations the Czaritsa sent out brought her any news of Safa Czarevich. From her people, throughout her vast land, came a silence as solemn, but as full of whisperings, as the silence within the Imperial Palace.

Those who had heard her proclamations laughed and said, 'Listen to our Czaritsa asking questions she knows the answers to! If she wants her nevvy back, why doesn't she go and dig him up from where she's buried him?'

But the Czaritsa really didn't know what had happened to her nephew. She suspected that people were hiding him, protecting him, and helping him to plan how to kill her and make himself Czar.

She sent soldiers to search the houses of her people. She sat awake at night, remembering people who had seemed to laugh at her, or people who had seemed sorry for the Czarevich. She wrote their names down in a long list, and soldiers went to their houses and smashed the doors, searched cupboards, tore floorboards up and panelling down.

But no Czarevich was found, however thorough the searches.

This did nothing to convince the Czaritsa that he was not to be found. She was the more convinced that he was being very cleverly hidden from her, and she ordered her army to search *every* house in the Czardom, even the smallest and poorest.

And still the Czarevich was not found. The Czaritsa was terrified. If her nephew was so clever that he could avoid all her attempts to catch him, how could he fail in his plan to murder her? She dreamt of him creeping out of the cold darkness, holding a knife, an axe, a cleaver.

She gave new orders to her soldiers. All those she had ever suspected of hiding the Czarevich would be arrested and executed, one by one, village by village, until her nephew was in her keeping.

Everyone in the Czardom, rich and poor, was afraid. Each of them thought to themselves, 'I don't know where Safa Czarevich is, but perhaps my neighbour does.' And people began to spy on their neighbours, relatives and friends. Was a family building a new room on their house? It must be a room for the Czarevich. People were heard moving about in the middle of the night? They must be secretly admitting the Czarevich to their home. Was there someone who had once been heard to say that the Czaritsa Margaretta was a cruel woman? Then surely that person was helping the Czarevich against his aunt.

Many heads were wastefully cut off before the bear came and ended the confusion.

The doors of the court-room opened, and through them came a bear. No one had seen it enter the Palace, no one had seen it in the passages, but in the court-room it was seen, snaking its head on its long neck, the fiercest of all bears, the white, northern bear.

Courtiers pressed back against the walls as the bear loped by to the steps of the Czar-chair. Its thick white fur ruffled as it moved, and a rank, wild-bear stink drove away the perfumes of the Palace. At the Czar-chair steps the bear suddenly rose on its hind legs and stood six feet tall.

Soldiers edged towards it, anxious not to draw its charge on themselves, but dutifully threatening it with pikes and spears.

The pikes and spears fell to the ground when the bear pushed back its head with its forepaws. The head fell back on its shoulders and the fur sagged away from its body. The bear – which the whole court had seen to be a bear – was now seen to be a burly man wearing a white bear's skin. He climbed the steps to the Czar-chair, and no one tried to stop him. The man was a witch.

The Czaritsa sat quite still and watched the man approach her. She was too afraid to rise from her chair, or to shout orders. Was this her nephew, she wondered, for she had never seen him. Were her nightmares coming true? A rank, greasy and bearish smell drifted to her from the slowly climbing figure.

A mass of hair and beard, all tabby-streaked grey and black, made the man's head seem large, while at the centre of all this hair his face was small, sharp and peering. It was Kuzma.

The shaman stopped in front of the Czar-chair and grinned at the Czaritsa. His sharp little face became all wrinkles; and seemed like a quick, fierce animal peering from a thicket and about to bite. 'I've come to offer you my help in finding your nephew, woman,' he said. 'You won't find him by your efforts, and you'll soon be ruler of nothing but bones and corpses. But I know where your nephew is.'

These were the words needed to help the Czaritsa recover her fear. With a noisy gasp of breath, she asked, 'Where is he?'

'He is under the protection of a shaman.'

'You?' the Czaritsa demanded.

'Another shaman, woman, not I. And if you call up every soldier in your Czardom, you won't be able to search the house of this shaman; and if you could search it, you wouldn't find your nephew, for she would turn him into gold and wear him in her ear, or into a plum-stone and hide him under her tongue. Nor could you kill her, not if you brought up all your cannon. You call yourself Czaritsa, and

you have power – but she is a Woman of Power.'
Kuzma grinned his sharp-faced grin. 'No, woman;
if you want your nephew returned to you, you must
have *my* help.'

'Stand back!' the Czaritsa ordered, and Kuzma
stood back while the Czaritsa rose to her feet and
rearranged the folds of her gold-encrusted skirts.
'My private apartments,' she said to her Captain of
Guards, and the Czaritsa and Kuzma were escorted
by armed soldiers through the palace to the
Czaritsa's apartments.

There they sat on low couches by the stove, and
tea was served to them. 'What reward are you
asking for your help?' said the Czaritsa.

'There is no reward *you* can give *me*, woman. I am
a shaman. I want only the death of the shaman who
protects the boy. Alone, I cannot hurt her. She
would smell out my lies. But with your help, I know
a way to kill her. Once she is dead, the boy is easily
taken.'

The Czaritsa ate a small cake, and said, 'But if all
my armies and my cannon cannot hurt her, of what
use is my help? How *can* she be killed?'

'Now, does one Czar tell everyone how easily he
killed his brother-Czars? Do you think I am going to
tell you how to kill another shaman?' Kuzma said.
'But give me a regiment of your soldiers, to
command as I like, and I will kill this shaman.'

'I don't lend my soldiers as a common housewife
lends flour,' said the Czaritsa. 'I must know that you
will succeed.'

112

'This is all I will tell you,' Kuzma said. 'A shaman can smell lies, and hear an untruth told, like a discord in music. If I set a trap of lies for my enemy, she will not come near it. The cries that draw her to it must be innocent and wholly truthful. Now; in your forests live a company of deserters – '

'Ah, those deserters!' the Czaritsa cried. 'I will have them executed!'

'I will execute them for you – once they have baited my trap,' said Kuzma. 'I will jangle them with fear. That will bring my enemy to me. Will you give me a regiment, woman, or will you not?'

The woman did; and that is all there is to tell of her for a while.

NINE

Round and round the tree goes the cat, its hard button paws treading down the grass.

In the forest, in the winter, says the cat, Vanya and his fellows live in hiding.

I am going to tell how Vanya's friends found an old man, a poor, nearly frozen traveller, in the forest; and took him to their village.

The stranger was lying in the snow near one of the soldiers' snares. They took him for a rich man – his coat was of thick, white bearskin. The fur of it was crusted with snow and rimed with frost. Even the hair of his black and grey beard was twisted into clear icicles, where his breath had frozen.

They tried to wake him, but he could only mutter in his cold sleep; and so they carried him to their village, where they crammed him into the crowded house where Vanya lived, close to the warmth of the stove.

People pushed close, and dragged the ice-covered bearskin from the man's body, for its thickness would keep the warmth from him if they left it on. As they lifted the man up, they heard a chinking, jingling sound coming from him. Vanya reached inside the man's shirt and pulled out a bag. He shook it and it made the sound of money.

While others opened the man's shirt to the warmth, and rubbed his hand and feet, Vanya opened the bag and shook some of the coins into his hand. They were copper coins, and each was stamped with the figure of a soldier, on both sides. One side showed the soldier from the front, and the other side the soldier from the back.

'Our foundling must be a foreigner,' Vanya said. 'I've never seen coins like these before.'

'When he wakes, we'll ask him where he comes from,' said someone.

But when the stranger was warm, and woke, and could talk – he answered no questions. He would not tell them his name, nor where he was from, nor how he had come to be freezing in the forest.

He ate nothing. When they offered him food, he said, 'That is not *my* kind of food.' He did not gossip, or tell stories, or play cards. All he did was to sit and count his copper coins, which he called 'my soldiers', saying, 'One soldier, two soldiers, three soldiers . . . '

He frightened the people. At first they thought him mad, and then they thought he was worse than that. How did he keep himself alive when he neither ate nor drank. *What* did he eat and drink, if not what they did?

The same night that the stranger was brought into the house, Vanya had a nightmare. He woke everyone with his cries, and even when he was shaken awake, he was trembling and sweating. In his dream, he said, he had seen the stranger come to his bedside – had seen it all very clearly! In the stranger's hand had been a knife, and this knife he had stabbed into Vanya's chest, and he had cut Vanya open as someone might split a loaf. It hadn't hurt, in the dream, Vanya said, but he had been terrified to look into his own body and see a glittering red stone, like a ruby, where his heart should have been. The stranger had taken hold of this red stone and had tried to wrench it from its place – but Vanya had woken before the stone had come loose.

No one can be blamed for what they do in other people's dreams, but this didn't make the villagers think more kindly of the stranger. And Vanya was ill the next day. He was weak and dizzy, and never left his bed. On the following day he did not even wake, but lay quite still, his body growing cooler, and his breathing less.

'Perhaps this time, the stone *was* pulled out,' someone said.

Others had the same dream; and others saw the glittering red stone within their own bodies and felt the stranger try to pull it out. And all those who had this dream became ill, just like Vanya.

There were five people lying ill in one house when the stranger came in and sat near the stove. He opened the bag where he kept his copper coins and, taking them out one by one, he counted them into stacks of ten, calling them soldiers. He had over a hundred soldiers. When he had them all piled up, he put his hand in the bag again and said, 'And five hearts.' From his hand he scattered five brightly coloured stones, like rubies, among the stacks of coins. He looked up at the frightened people, laughed, and vanished, popped out of sight like a burst bubble.

But though he was no longer seen, he was not gone. The people heard him in the house with them, counting his soldiers and hearts; and they went on having the nightmares he had brought to them, and more and more people fell sick.

They feared they were being haunted by a ghost or demon that meant to kill them by entering their dreams and attacking them inside their sleep. In fear, they prayed for help; in fear they went about their work; in fear they lay awake at night.

All their fear went out of them and travelled ringing in the air. Kuzma could hear it as he sat invisibly in a corner of the house. And he knew that Chingis would hear it.

TEN

Listen, says the cat. I am going to tell of Chingis again.

Chingis heard the fear of the villagers. As she sat by the stove in her house on chicken-legs, learning from the books her witch-mother had left her, the shrilling of fear in the air was something unheard that made her shudder suddenly, for no cause, and look up.

She had set Safa to study letters. 'Do you hear it?' she asked. Willingly, he raised his head and listened, and there was so much to hear! Their own breathing, softly mixing with the gentle sounds of the fire burning in the stove; the many different creaking joints of the hut, the frost crackling about the roof, the wind in the house-corners and in the trees – but none of these sounds were what Chingis heard.

She came and set a hand on his shoulder and, leaning her head close to his, raised a finger. 'Listen,' she said. He closed his eyes and held his breath, and all that he did besides was to let his heart beat. Still he could not hear what she heard, but suddenly he shook, from head to foot, for no reason. He was not cold.

'Someone has trodden on my grave,' he said, for that was what Marien had always said when she shuddered.

'It is fear,' said Chingis, 'but not the fear of hunger.' She listened, and her tongue poked from between her teeth, as if she tasted the sound. 'It is a fear of death, but not only of death,' she said. 'Something frightens these people – but what? A bear? A ghost?' She slapped Safa's shoulder. 'The drum!'

Safa fetched the shaman-drum from the wall. They sat on the stove-shelf and he held the drum across his knees while she placed the skull at its centre and began the steady drumming.

Safa hardly blinked as he watched the skull slide and skip from symbol to symbol. He guessed at what each jump might mean, but none of his guesses made sense. He had learned some of the symbols' meanings, but not all of them, nor anything of the meanings that connected one sign to another. For him, trying to understand the drum was like trying to read a word when you know the names of the letters but not the sounds they make.

Chingis stopped drumming, and Safa looked to her, expecting to be told what the drum had said. But she said, 'The drum tells me nothing.' She was puzzled, Safa saw. 'It tells me nothing,' she said.

But she could still hear the fear in the air. It thrummed in her bones and crawled over her skin like cold water droplets, drawing shivers from her.

'We shall go to them,' she said; but as she laid the drum aside, she said, 'It tells me nothing. I don't know why.'

The house raised itself on its chicken-legs and walked, carrying them inside it, towards the place where the fear was.

Listen (says the cat) and I'll tell you of Kuzma.

Kuzma sat on the stove in Vanya's house. All around him, on the stove and on the floor, lay the people of that house, scarcely breathing. Some were so cold, and so still, as they stared with dusty, open eyes into the darkness of the roof, that they might have been already dead.

In the other two houses of the village, it was the same. A softly breathed word, now and then, could be heard from someone still warm enough to moan – but they were chilling and freezing and becoming immovable.

In Kuzma's bag, with the copper coins he called his soldiers, rattled many glittering red stones.

Warm and safe as he sat cross-legged on the stove, Kuzma sent out his spirit. It flew about and between the forest trees as fast as snowflakes carried on a gust of wind. It flew to the topmost points of the tall pine-trees as fast as he thought himself there. And it looked about and listened, and looked about – and saw Chingis coming from far off.

Back to its body flew Kuzma's spirit, and Kuzma opened his eyes.

'Quick! Quick!' he said to himself, and jumped from the stove. Out of the house he went, and ran, quick, quick, quick, away into the trees, stumbling in his heavy boots and the deep snow.

Far from the houses he stopped, near an over-hanging bank where snow had drifted. He wrapped himself closely in his coat made of a white bear's skin, and drew over his head the bear's head. He rolled himself into the snow and curled himself up, and sank himself into the deepest of sleeps. Like a hibernating bear his heart beat slower and slower, his body grew cooler. There was so little life in his body that he hardly existed; and his spirit had gone to stand outside the gates of the ghost-world. Was it a man or a bear who slept there in the snow? Or no living thing at all, but merely a snow-covered log?

As the house on chicken-legs approached the village, the sound of fear that it followed dropped and faded. Again Chingis questioned her drum; again it told her nothing. She was suspicious and wary, and the house came to a halt while it was still at a distance from the village. The drum said that the village was empty; that no living soul was there. To Safa, Chingis said, 'Here: hold my hand, little brother, and don't be afraid.' He took her hand and held it tightly; and she closed her eyes and sent out her spirit.

It was in the village in an instant, and whisked in and out of the houses like a draught under their doors. She saw the people, dead, but not dead.

Up the stove pipes, spiralling – out and high into

the cold air – in half a moment her spirit looked down on the tops of the pine-trees – but she neither saw, heard, smelled nor felt a trace of anything that might have caused the people's strange sickness. Kuzma had hidden himself well.

Chingis flew high and scanned far. She came to earth and hunted round the tree-boles like a little, nimble weasel. But, for all her skill, she was a young shaman, and had not grown crafty and wary of such tricks as Kuzma's. He was well hidden and she had overlooked him.

And Safa began to be afraid of her body's white, rolled-back eyes, and its strange breathing and trembling. He began to call her name. Back she went to her body, to make its eyes dark again, and to reassure him that she was safe.

The hut on chicken-legs carried them to the centre of the village; and they left it and went into the three legless houses.

Kuzma heard them, deep in his sleep. His heart began to beat faster; warmth once more spread through his body. He stirred and rose, snow-covered, from the snow where he had hidden. Quickly he made his way back to the village, knowing that Chingis would be thinking only of the people in the houses, and would not be on her guard against him.

In Vanya's house, Chingis said to Safa, 'These are bodies without souls – they are not dead or dying.'

'Give them their souls back,' Safa said.

'But why have their spirits left them?' Chingis

said. She looked about, and listened. 'Or have they been stolen? Little brother – we may be in danger!'

Outside the house, in the milky darkness, stood the shaman, Kuzma.

He opened the bag he carried and took out the copper coins. He walked round the village, scattering the coins on the snow. The soldier stamped on the coins stamped, and became a real soldier. Every soldier had a trumpet, as well as weapons, and every soldier had bunches of bells tied round his waist, ankles and wrists.

The hut on chicken-legs began to stamp its taloned feet, and to make strange cackling, crackling noises, like a chicken, or like a fire. It raked up the snow and banged its outer door. Chingis heard it, and she came out of Vanya's house, leading Safa by the hand. As soon as she appeared, the soldiers began to blow their trumpets, or to yell; to stamp their feet and set their bells jangling.

The noise they made was so loud, nothing else could be heard – and the soldiers could hear nothing anyway. Their ears were plugged tight.

A shaman's power is all words and music. If she cannot be heard, her power is niggling.

Chingis raised her voice and yelled so loud that the words scraped her throat raw on the way out. She yelled words that would have locked the soldiers' limbs as solidly as so many statues, if they had been able to hear her. But they could not hear her, and they had swords and knives.

Safa didn't understand what he was seeing. Here

were more soldiers like those who guarded his dome-room – but they were noisier than other soldiers. He could see Chingis shouting at them, but could not hear what she was saying. He knew that knives were sharp and drew blood, and these soldiers were holding long knives – but he had little understanding of the harm people can do one another. He stood and watched, and while he watched five soldiers came to him. They pushed him face down in the snow and tied his hands. All the while the bells tied to them jangled and rang in a patternless din; and trumpets and yells added to the row.

When the soldiers pulled him to his feet, he looked for Chingis, but couldn't see her. Soldiers were in his way. Between their bodies and legs he saw red snow. The noise was less now; no trumpets and yelling, but only the thrashing of the bells as the soldiers moved. Safa watched the scarlet colour creep rapidly through the snow-crystals, losing colour as it ran, until it was no more than white touched with pink. And then, with a din of bells, a party of soldiers ran up, bringing a long pole, sharpened at one end. The other soldiers scattered to make way for them, and Safa saw, through the gap, Chingis lying at the centre of the scarlet and pink stain. He called to her, called and called, as his spirit had once called, but she didn't move or turn to him.

Then he saw a man in a white bearskin coat take the pole and set its sharpened end on Chingis's chest. The man took a hammer from a soldier, and raised it to drive the sharpened pole home. Safa yelled and told him no, he must not – but the sound of the hammer blows banged dully through the light tingling of the bells the soldiers wore, and the pole was driven in, fixing Chingis's body to the ground.

'Now she won't come walking after dark, following after us,' said the man in the white bearskin, and the soldiers laughed, and took a few steps as they laughed, so their bells rang again.

'Now you may be the greatest shaman in the ghost-world,' Kuzma said to Chingis, 'but I won't be in the ghost-world for a while yet!' To the soldiers, he said, 'Tidy up this place, lads!'

The soldiers fetched fire from the houses, and used the fire to set the houses burning. With ropes, they tripped the house on chicken-legs, set fire to its shingle-roof and destroyed it. When the village was ruined and flaming, the soldiers left, taking Safa with them. The ringing of the bells they wore amused them as they marched along and Kuzma sang them songs in a loud, deep voice. After they'd heard his songs, they forgot why it was they were wearing the bells and carrying trumpets, and how they had killed the witch. All they could clearly remember was that they had destroyed a village of traitors that had been hiding the Czarevich; and now they had recaptured the Czarevich and were taking him back to the Imperial City, where their Holy Czaritsa would reward them.

At the end of their journey the soldiers escorted Safa Czarevich into the Holy Presence of his aunt. She sat, waiting, high on her Czar-chair, her guards and courtiers gathered below. The Czaritsa rose from her chair and descended its steps in a cascade of gold-shot silk and shining jewels. She came down almost to the level of ordinary people, put her arms round the dirty boy in his feather-decked robe, and kissed his face.

'Safa, darling,' she said, pinching his cheek, 'you shall never again wander out of my reach. But you need clean clothes and a long rest. Guards! Escort the Czarevich to the apartment prepared for him.'

As soon as the Czarevich had been taken away, and Margaretta had climbed back to the Czar-chair, Kuzma pushed his way through the courtiers and mounted its steps. He had a leather bag in his hand, and when he reached the Czaritsa he up-ended the bag and emptied the contents into her lap. Out fell many bright, red, glittering stones.

Without a word, Kuzma vanished. He had gained what he wished – the death of Chingis.

The Holy, Compassionate Czaritsa Margaretta was much taken with the red stones Kuzma had given her. They were a darker and richer crimson than any rubies she had ever seen, and glittered in the candlelight with the intensity of frost crystals.

'Now that my beloved nephew is being taken care of,' said the Czaritsa, 'and I have no more reason to fear the traitors within my Czardom, now I can truly celebrate my coronation. In the Cathedral of the Czaritsa of the Sorrows I shall be crowned with a new crown, that no Czar or Czaritsa has worn before me. I shall have it set with these stones.' And she held up one of the red stones so that all might see how it glared when it caught the light.

It is strange that, being so untrustworthy herself, the Czaritsa trusted Kuzma, and accepted his gift: perhaps she thought he had recaptured Safa for love of her.

The crown was made, a magnificent thing, and was set with the red stones by slave-craftsmen. It was placed on the head of the Czaritsa Margaretta in the Cathedral, near the tomb of her dead sister-in-law. At every state occasion the Czaritsa proudly wore it – the crown set with the souls of her subjects.

But what had happened to the Czarevich?

The apartment prepared for him is the dome-room at the top of the highest tower in the Imperial Palace. There are guards outside the locked door, and guards on the stairs, and guards at the foot of the stairs.

Nothing has been done to the dome-room since Vanya and the other soldiers tore it apart. It is dark, and utterly bare. It holds nothing but the stove, the floorboards, the brick of the walls – and the unfortunate, the lonely Safa Czarevich.

But Safa's spirit has learned the ways out of the dome-room.

It often happens that you understand what was said to you only long after it was spoken; or that you remember clearly things you saw, but never noticed, while they were before your eyes.

Safa had been an unteachable apprentice, unable to learn the simplest word-magics while he had been surrounded by the clamour, glamour and clutter of our world.

But in the dark, empty silence of the dome-room, he remembered what had been said to him; and saw what had been shown to him. In the long silence, he put word to picture, and picture to word, and made a whole of them.

In long dreams his spirit travelled, to places in this world, and to places in other worlds. It turned back only from the gate of the ghost-world. He was as afraid to step through that gate as most of us are.

Safa was no shaman – but he was learning to be a witch.

ELEVEN

The cat stops pacing round the tree, and sits and licks its paws.

Is this the end of the story? asks the cat. With Chingis dead and Safa captured, with Margaretta crowned and celebrated as All-Powerful Czaritsa, how can the story go on except with Safa's execution and Margaretta's ruling for ever and ever?

The story goes on (says the cat) by telling more of Chingis, dead though she is.

When we sleep, the eyes of our body close, and we see this world no longer. But the eyes of our spirits open wide, and let in all the sights of other worlds.

When the eyes of Chingis's body closed in death, the eyes of her spirit started open, as from a nightmare. All the senses of her spirit tingled sharp and clear.

She looked into a darkness barred with the trunks of trees. From the darkness came a singing – perhaps of birds, but it was unlike birds – a singing of such slow, distant sadness that it slowed the heart and chilled the skin.

(For Chingis still felt a heart beat within her, and a covering of skin over her, just as we all do when we dream.)

From the darkness of the trees, with the singing, came drifting the deep-toned sea-scent of rosemary and thyme, and a darker, ashy stink of burning.

She was alone. All the noise and din of the soldiers, the companionship of Safa, all had vanished. Chingis turned and found a high gate behind her. She knew it; she knew it for the gate of the ghost-world.

Always, before, she had come to the gate, and opened it with words, and gone in; but now she was already on the other side of the gate. It was closed and locked behind her. No words would open it.

So Chingis knew that she was dead.

She had travelled to the ghost-world many, many times, but when the gate would not open for her, and she found herself trapped there, she felt the sickness of fear. But she said aloud, 'I am a shaman!' And she said to herself the shaman proverb that her witch-mother had taught her: 'Whenever you poke your nose round the door, take courage with you.'

The forest ahead of her was Iron-Wood, which is not a good place or a bad place, but good or bad, according to how you travel it.

Chingis walked forward, came among crowds of people, women, children, and men, people sitting, lying, standing, all gathered at the edges of the Iron-Wood's heavy trees, afraid to go further. The trees of

130

that wood shone dimly, reflecting the dullest of iron-grey light. Their leaves, when they moved, clanked together like iron keys on iron locks. Their branches were cold and clung to the skin like freezing metal; and the scent that came from these trees was not a smell of earth or sap, but the cold, dull smell of metal things. Most frightening of all was the singing which wove through the iron trees, too fine to be that of birds, too unknowing to be human.

The people saw Chingis pass through them and walk among the trees. Some of them took courage from her, and followed, but they soon lost sight of her and of each other. Iron-Wood has no paths. A way must be chosen between the trees – this way, now that, now this, with no guide.

But Chingis knew who and what she sought, and her way through Iron-Wood was marked as plain as if a road had been cleared. She could no more wander than a magnet can wander on its way to the iron that pulls it; at each tree she could no more doubt the way to turn than the magnet can doubt where the iron lies. She passed so swiftly through the wood that her feet hardly touched the iron leaves that piled the forest floor, and the only sound of her going was a faint one, like the slow settling of iron nails in a box.

When she came where she meant to be, she saw the hut on chicken-legs crouching under the pressing, heavy shelter of iron branches and iron leaves. Standing outside it was her witch-mother, who saw her coming and held open her arms, warm arms that folded about Chingis and hugged her tightly; warm hands that drummed lovingly on Chingis's back.

'When my old house came to me here, I knew you would soon come following after,' said the old witch. 'I have questioned the drum – I know all that happened – it was Kuzma! It was Kuzma, the traitor, who taught the soldiers how to kill a shaman.'

'Grandmother, did you question the drum about my apprentice?'

'You have no apprentice,' the old witch said.

'I have: I took him from prison. He was not chosen as you chose me, and he is not teachable, but I care for him. Was he killed too, Grandmother? Is he here, lost in Iron-Wood?'

'He was not killed,' said the old woman, 'but I know nothing more of him.'

'Then question the drum again, Grandmother.'

The old witch's shaman-drum lay on the iron leaves near the house on chicken-legs. The old witch sat on a rusting iron log and set the drum across her knees. She began drumming and Chingis, crouching beside her, watched the movements of the weasel's skull.

Chingis's sight was darkened by the darkness of Safa's prison, though he was worlds away. She felt the looming closeness of the dome-room's enclosing wall; the silence of the prison swamped her hearing as if she sank in water. She felt, saw, sensed all this faintly, but clearly – just as we, reading a book, see

132

the scene painted thinly and faintly between our eyes and the page.

When the drumming stopped there were four women gathered round the drum in the dull, iron light of Iron-Wood, beneath its heavy branches. There was the old witch and there was Chingis. And there was a third, a worn and anxious woman; and a fourth, a tall and beautiful woman with long dark hair and large dark eyes. They were Marien, the nurse, and Farida, the slave-Czaritsa. Chingis looked at them, and knew at once who they were, and that the drum's talk of Safa had brought them there.

'Grandmother, I must leave this world and go into the old one again,' Chingis said.

The old witch shook her head. 'You are dead now, daughter.'

'I come and go between the worlds as I wish!' Chingis said.

'A fish lives in water, but in air it dies,' said the old witch. 'A spirit can live in the spirit-worlds, but on earth a spirit is soon blown to pieces unless it has a body to creep back to and take shelter. Your body is dead and turning to dust, Chingis.'

'I'll go back into it.'

'It will be cold by now, and too heavy to move. Kuzma has pinned it to the ground.'

'I must and shall go back to earth,' Chingis said. 'If I cannot go into my old body, I'll go into another.'

'Into what body?' asked the old woman. 'Whatever living body you enter, you will have to fight with the spirit that already shelters there. That spirit will never rest while you are in its home. You will waste your strength in battling. It's no use, daughter. Even a shaman, once dead, must wait until another body has grown to house her. At the centre of Iron-Wood you may see them growing, on the ash. This Safa you call your apprentice will have been dead for centuries before you see earth again.'

Chingis's head drooped, but Marien the nurse and Farida the slave-woman each laid a hand on her shoulders.

'If I can help you – ' said Marien.

'And if I can help you – ' said Farida.

Chingis raised her head and said, 'Grandmother, if four spirits went into my old body, could they raise and move it with the strength of them all?'

'If none of those spirits has eaten the Iron-Wood fruit,' said the old witch.

'I have eaten nothing in this place,' said Farida. 'I left my child in a prison, and thinking of his poor life keeps me full with grief.'

'I was more a mother to him than his mother,' said Marien, the nurse, 'and through my foolishness, I left him alone in the dark . . . Do you think I care to eat?'

'And you've drunk no water from these rusty streams?' the old witch asked.

The two ghosts shook their heads.

'And you, Grandmother? Have you eaten? Have you drunk?'

The old witch sighed, and smiled, and put a hard,

creased hand on Chingis's cheek. 'I have missed my daughter,' she said, and shook her head.

'Then you will help us find the way through the Iron-Wood and back to earth, Grandmother!'

'We cannot return through the gate now,' said the old witch. 'It's locked against us. We must find our way through Iron-Wood at its wildest . . . and if we lose our way we may never find it again.'

'Whenever you poke your nose out of doors, pack courage, Grandmother, and leave fear at home.'

The old witch smiled. 'Leave the drum, leave the house. We can take nothing from here except courage. Take my hands – we must all hold hands and never be parted, for only two of us can find our way. Chingis – my strong daughter, Chingis – you must lead. If you cannot make this journey, then none of us can. And I will come last, and when you lose the way, I will call it out to you.'

And so Chingis, and Marien, and Farida, and the old witch, began the long travelling through Iron-Wood, through iron thorns and steel briars, from the ghost-world to earth.

TWELVE

Now I shall bring my story back to this world, says the cat, and tell of the All-Compassionate, Ever-Ruling, Newly Crowned Czaritsa Margaretta.

Her thoughts often climbed the stairs of the Czarevich Tower to the room where her nephew was imprisoned, but, wherever her thoughts went, the Czaritsa remained seated on her Czar-chair, wearing her crown set with crimson and scarlet stones. And always she saw, to the side and behind her, white pillars, white figures, standing too close.

No one should be standing near the Czar-chair; no one was allowed to climb the Czar-chair steps. No one had been allowed. Yet there those white pillars stood; and when she rolled her eyes far to the side, she saw they were people. When she turned her head to see them clearly, they shrank back, crumpled and vanished, as reflections in a distorting mirror crumple and vanish when you move.

The Czaritsa knew that these vague figures at the edge of her vision were not real, solid people: so she did not order her soldiers to remove them. She did not mention them, but sat upright and still, her red-glittering crown on her head, peering from the corners of her eyes.

As she walked through the Palace with her escort of soldiers, the Czaritsa passed mirror after mirror; and in those mirrors she saw naked people standing closer to her than any of her soldiers stood. Naked, starving, snow-white men and women; reflected, starving children. As her eyes turned to the mirror, their eyes turned to hers. But these naked souls could not be heard or touched, or seen outside the glass.

I see ghosts, thought the Czaritsa to herself, but she determined to ignore them. Ghosts can stare and ghosts can hate, but mere spirits without body can do no harm in this world.

The ghosts took her thoughts away with their staring. She thought they must be the ghosts of people she had ordered to be executed – she had not realized there had been so many executions.

The Czaritsa had every mirror in the Palace taken down and smashed to pieces, even those in her private apartments. The broken shards of glass she had ground into powder; and the powder she had poured into jars and put away in the Palace storerooms, for sprinkling on the food of her enemies. Though a Czaritsa, she was a thoughtful and thrifty housewife.

No longer seen in the mirrors, the ghosts were still there, and the Czaritsa could not prevent herself from rolling her eyes sidelong to see them, any more than we can keep from touching a sore place in our mouths to see if it is still sore. The ghosts no longer shrank back from her sight. They advanced and stood plainly before her eyes even as she sat on the Czar-chair in her court-room.

At night she was alone with them in her apartments. However long she kept her maids and her slaves about her, at last she must send them away, or admit that she was afraid to be alone – and what God on earth can admit that? With her wig taken off and her grey hair let down; with her heavy, spreading, bejewelled dress packed away and only a thin nightgown to cover her spongy old limbs, she must crawl over the width of the Imperial Bed, like a lost traveller crawling over a snow-plain, to huddle in the middle of its expanse and stare back at the staring skeletons gathered all round her.

The Palace was always silent: at night there was not the slightest breath of sound to distract or encourage. The Czaritsa was at her weakest, and could no longer look into the ghosts' hunger-bruised eyes. She hid her face, she wept, she prayed for them to be taken away – but when she looked again, they still stared.

'If I ordered your deaths, then that is how your deaths were fated,' she said. 'I have a mandate from God! Nothing I can do is wrong!'

The ghosts stared.

'You are commanded to forgive me,' the Czaritsa told them. 'Great folk like me must often do dreadful things – they must, you know they must, to make the world go. So, you see, you are not to blame me.'

The ghosts did not seem to hear her. They were with her the next day and the next night. Their faces did not blame. They only stared their hunger.

Why had they not gone away, the Czaritsa wondered. Were they such unchristian ghosts that they had no forgiveness? Or were they not haunting her for revenge at all?

There are a thousand stories of ghosts returning to this world to tell the living of treasure buried, or to beg for some wrong they had done during life to be put right. And, remembering these stories, the Czaritsa understood at once that the ghosts had not come to blame her, but to beg her to do something she had left undone.

And what had she not done?

She had not killed her nephew.

High in the dome-room at the top of the Imperial Palace's highest tower, Safa Czarevich still lived. In darkness, in loneliness, but still he breathed and his heart beat.

Who knew what plans he was making up there, whispering to his guards through the keyhole?

She had not been as thorough as a Czaritsa should be; and the ghosts of her beloved people had come to warn her of her danger.

Tears filled her eyes at this proof of how much her people loved her. There were a few treacherous, twisted, unnatural people among her subjects who hated her and worked against her – but most of her people, thank God, were true, loyal and decent, and loved her so much that they returned from the dead to warn her against danger, and to beg her to take action to save herself.

'Thank you for your care – I bless you!' the Czaritsa said to them. 'I promise you, I shall do as you advise. I shall kill him. Yes, I shall send him to join you. He can stand among you and stare at me too. Axes and knives draw blood. A stare never made anyone bleed.'

The ghosts showed no pleasure or displeasure. They merely stood and stared.

'When he is dead,' said the Czaritsa, 'I shall give him such a funeral that everyone will say, "How she must have loved him! How she must have suffered when she was forced to order his death!" They will make songs about it – the Suffering of the Czaritsa Margaretta!' She sighed as she thought of the beautiful coffin she would have made; of the songs and the ceremony – and the magnificent tomb she would build for the Czarevich between the tombs of his mother and father. There she would go daily to weep for her nephew. How pitiful she would look! How her people would grieve for her when they saw her sorrowing.

The ghosts stared at her without any sorrow.

When a poor woman wishes a troublesome relative dead, it is rarely more than a passing wish, however sincere.

But when a Czaritsa has the same wish, you may be sure the wish will come true.

THIRTEEN

Now, what shall I tell next? asks the cat.

In the silent, lacquered, gilded, half-lit maze of the Palace, the Czaritsa sits awake at night, and tells her funeral plans to unlistening ghosts. She orders solemn music to be written; she orders tomb-makers to work; she orders a gown for herself, to be so closely sewn with jet beads that it will seem made of coal, not cloth. She does not say whose funeral she prepares for: but everyone knows.

Far above the Palace, wrapped in darkness by the brick of the dome, like a mite in a nutshell, is Safa, though he is not always there in spirit.

But now I know what to tell, says the cat. The story shall go on with the bear-shaman, Kuzma, and the dead shaman, Chingis.

Kuzma's house stood on chicken-legs too, but the legs were bones.

Kuzma was in his house, was in his bed, asleep and dreaming. In his dream he saw a river of scarlet water which drove along bones instead of driftwood. He looked across the width of the river to the dimness of its other bank, where the grey and clanking trees of Iron-Wood were reflected, red and black, in the river.

In his dream Kuzma walked by the river and watched its other bank. He watched it fearfully, as someone alone in darkness fearfully watches the trees about him for something he dreads to see, but is more afraid of not seeing. And something came out of the Iron-Wood and stared over the river at Kuzma.

Kuzma peered through the darkness. He saw four figures under the iron trees, and the leading figure was Chingis, made ragged by steel thorns. She had a bow slung on her shoulder, and a quiver of arrows. Fitting an arrow to her bow string, she came wading into the river, aiming at Kuzma. When the red water was about her thighs, and the drifting bones were catching against her hip, she shot her arrow. It flew high over the river, but curved down, and plunged into the red water.

Kuzma woke into this world, still feeling the cold, creeping dread which had come to him in the dream. The meaning of it was clear: Chingis was dead, but she would harm him if she could. She was at the borders of the ghost-world, and she was seeking a way to leave it.

Kuzma knew that no spirit can come safely to earth without a body to shelter it. Chingis would try to reach him in one of the other worlds, where her spirit would fight against his while his body slept.

That Kuzma would not allow. He was afraid to meet Chingis spirit to spirit. He feared her strength and anger. He would not fight Chingis unless she was in such difficulties that he could not fail to win.

Kuzma was an old man. He needed little sleep. From the rafters of his house he took herbs and roots and made distillations of them, to keep himself from sleeping. If he never slept, then his spirit could not wander in dreams, and Chingis would be forced to meet him in this world; and to do that she would have to enter a body. Then she would have two fights: the fight with Kuzma, and the fight against the spirit whose body she had stolen.

Kuzma's dread faded as he grew sure of winning. He drank his wakeful drink and shouted aloud, 'Come then, Chingis, and I'll make an end of you, world within world!'

For a whole month of nights, Kuzma kept his house in the same place, drank his wakeful drink, and watched and listened for any creature that might approach him. A thousand times he thought the wait was over and leapt up to save himself. A thousand times he found the battle was not yet.

Even Kuzma began to tire. He added other herbs to his wakeful drink, and it gave him strength for a few hours. Those few hours over, he was more weak and tired than before. Every sip of his drink took a year off his life, and it seemed that Chingis was killing him without coming near him.

He feared there was some cleverness in Chingis's delay that he could not guess. He could only hope that she would come soon, in some shape he could trap, or maim, or kill.

When the house around him began to scream and cackle, then he knew that someone was near. He poured a bowlful of wakeful drink, drank it all, and went to the door.

In the snow outside stood Chingis's dead body, upright, walking. In its dead hand, it carried an axe.

Kuzma's heart squeezed small and tight with such fear as he had not known for a hundred and fifty years. Here was why Chingis had been so long in coming. The corpse had risen from the place where it had died and had walked over the land, step by heavy step, in search of Kuzma. Kuzma had thought only shamans in legends had spirits so strong.

But Kuzma smiled and sat on his doorstep, as if corpses with axes visited him every day. 'Well, well, little daughter,' he said. 'You know a way from the ghost-world that I don't know.' Kuzma hoped to win by cunning if he couldn't win by strength; he hoped to trick Chingis into telling what she should keep secret. 'You are a greater shaman than I knew,' he said. 'How is it possible that you come here, dressed in the dead?'

Chingis answered him, and Kuzma listened gladly. Her words slithered and slobbered from her body's cold, rigid mouth. 'I stood at the borders of the ghost-world and earth, where the spirits slip by and enter thoughts and dreams. I could see my body lying where you had pinned it to the ground, and I saw wolves and birds come to it, to eat it. I was angry, and I slipped easily into the angry minds of those gobblers – but before they knew I was in them, I slipped out again and into my old body. Oh, it was a cold house, Kuzma – cold and lightless. Before I could force open the eyes and see the light of this world – look! the wolf had eaten my arm.'

Chingis made her body hold out its right arm, which was nothing but bones and shreds.

'And it was hard work, Kuzma, to make the tongue in here beat on the teeth like a wooden paddle on rocks. To raise the head was as easy as raising a boulder on a blade of grass. What labour! But I am strong, Kuzma. I raised up the head, I made the tongue speak, and I drove away the wolf and the birds. Then I made these hands, these arms, drag out the stake you had driven through me. I raised this body, this long, tall body – I raised it to its feet. Easier to make a necklace of rocks stand upright! I thought it would end me – but the thought of telling you this, Kuzma, drove me to succeed . . . I took this axe from the village you burned. See, its edge is a little spoiled by the fire, but it is still sharp. This dead body has not stopped or lain down since I raised it up. It has done nothing but turn its nose towards you and put one foot before the other. My grandmother advised me to tell you all this, Kuzma. She said it would make your blood almost as cold as mine – and I see by your colour that it has.'

'You have your axe,' Kuzma said. 'Let me go inside and fetch mine.'

He rose and went into his house. The corpse let him go.

Inside his house, Kuzma took his axe and stuck its shaft through his belt; took a shaman-drum from the wall and slung it on his shoulder. From a shelf he took a jar and filled his mouth with the powder it contained – a powder which filled him with strength. Over himself – over the drum and axe and all – he drew the white bear's skin, while he muttered a pattern of words. His body twisted under the bear skin and became a bear's body. In bear-shape he sprang from the door of his hut, sprang past Chingis, and loped away over the snow with long, heavy strides. Kuzma hoped to save his life for another day.

But as the bear leaped away from the hut, a small, spiked seed-head, trailing a length of dried stick, drifted into the bear's fur and clung there. Chingis had crushed her corpse and all its indwelling spirits to this seed, and the stick the seed trailed was the axe.

She could not stay so small for long, and had to change her shape: and she changed it to a leech, a big leech, that reached through thick fur to the bear's skin and sucked on its blood.

Kuzma had not felt the bur catch or the leech bite, and he ran on, thinking himself safe. The weakness which sickened his heart and trembled in his bones, he thought mere weariness.

As Kuzma grew weaker, Chingis grew stronger; and the powder that had made Kuzma strong now flowed in his blood from him to Chingis. The leech swelled. The bear's legs ceased to move and shook beneath the bear's weight; its head dropped to the snow. Now Chingis reappeared in her own shape, sitting astride the bear and raising the axe above her head.

Kuzma cowered under the blow that killed him. The two bodies, the one dead, the other dying, fell and rolled in the snow. As Kuzma rolled, the bearskin opened and showed the man inside. Chingis leaned over him and put her mouth to his, as if she kissed him.

Kuzma's spirit rose to leave his dying body; but its way was stopped and it was overwhelmed by the entrance of spirits from Chingis's kiss.

Those four long-travelled spirits who had found their way through Iron-Wood pounced on the spirit that only wished to escape. They trapped it, wrapped it, in nets of hair and air, in words and music. They carried it, prisoner, far into another world. They made it prisoner in a cage of wooden sticks, in a cave blocked by a boulder, in a bottle stopped by a cork, in a coffin of glass. The spirit of the old witch was left to guard Kuzma's, while the others filled their new spirit-house and joined their strength together to move it.

Kuzma's body was still warm and fresh. It moved easily to the will of the new spirits that inhabited it. Rising, it looked down on the dead body of Chingis.

Kuzma's body walked, with only a slight clumsiness, a short distance away. Turning, it looked back with Kuzma's eyes, but Chingis's sight. From the trees a wolf came scuttling to the corpse.

Kuzma's house, on its skeletal legs, knew that Kuzma was coming home to it, but sensed that it was not truly Kuzma. It began to cluck and cackle, and shut its doors, but opened them again when Chingis, speaking through Kuzma's mouth, ordered them to open. The house was only a house. It could do nothing to prevent its master's dead, but walking, body from entering.

Inside the rafters were hung with herbs, the shelves stocked with jars, the walls hung with drums, with flutes, with mandolins. On the table lay a large, plain wooden box. Curious, Chingis opened it with Kuzma's hand.

The box held ice-apples. Their cold rose from them in a chill, apple-scented mist. The apples seemed made of glass. Their skins were transparent and so pale a green as to be colourless.

The flesh was transparent, though the light trapped within the apples made the transparency milky. Juice sparkled in droplets, like frost.

At the heart of the apples, hanging in space, could be seen the flower-tracery of the cores, and the black pips.

Chingis lifted an apple by its stalk – in Kuzma's fingers – and turned it. The dark pips whirled. The apple gathered to itself all the light there was, and shone without heat; shone dimly and softly, like light seen through water, a light coloured with the faint, barely visible green seen in snow.

Ice-apples are rare. Compared to them, diamonds are as common as sand grains on a beach. Unicorns are more easily found than ice-apples. Yet here was a box of them, shining like moonlight on a night of rain.

Kuzma's hand moved and placed the ice-apple it held inside the white bearskin coat, laying the ice-apple against the icy heart.

FOURTEEN

Now I'll tell of a funeral procession, says the cat.

The Imperial Palace was a city with one roof; but most cities are full of noise and lights. The Imperial Palace had always a breath-held silence, and twilight.

Through this dim silence soldiers came marching. Was it day or night? In the Palace, day and night came according to orders. Candlelight turns many rich colours to black, and the soldiers' uniforms seemed black on black with belts of black. To the stealthy sounds of candles burning, to the creak and clink of belts and swords, and the shush of thick-soled boots on carpets and stone, the soldiers climbed the stairs of the highest tower and opened the dome-room door.

Safa Czarevich was waiting for them. His eyes were dazzled by even so feeble a light as candlelight, but he went with them willingly and, as he went, he nodded his head and glanced about as if he followed the rhythm of music. The Palace was silent. There was no music. But the Czarevich was mad, as everyone knew.

Down the stairs and by silent corridors they

marched, until they reached broader corridors where dragons and flowers were painted over the walls and ceiling, glowing a sudden rich red and green where they were close to a stand of candles. Here the soldiers met priests in tall hats and stiff black robes; and boys dressed in white, swinging gold fire-cans of burning incense on gold chains. Here was the executioner, his heavy axe on his shoulder. His clothes seemed brown, but flared suddenly into scarlet when the full light of the candles fell on them. Beside the executioner was carried the coffin, reflecting everything near it, as dark water does, and shimmering along its length each time it was carried beneath a clump of candles.

Through other corridors, as silently, came the Czaritsa Margaretta and her guard, and her ghosts. The Czaritsa's black gown was so closely sewn over with jet beads that it clashed as she walked, and seemed to have no cloth in it. The ghosts were so close to her that they trod on the hem of the beaded gown – but their tread had no weight.

The Czaritsa peered sidelong at them, but would then remember the execution she was going to attend, and pause to sob and wipe her eyes. Quickly she would look about her to see if her loving soldiers were admiring her grief, and would tell others of it later. She could already hear the story they would tell being told in her own head: how the compassionate Czaritsa was so filled with love and care for her people that she had her own nephew executed, though she loved him, to save her people

151

from his wicked treachery. What a sacrifice! What a strong, loving mother to her people she was, hiding her pain and sorrow for their sake. And she wiped her eyes again, and peeped again at her soldiers.

In the court-room the courtiers waited for the arrival of the Czaritsa, and of the Czarevich who was to be executed. The courtiers stood staring up at the Czar-chair. Smoke from the candles curled and drifted gauzily through the candlelight, and hung in clouds under the dark roof. The painted windows showed their darkest, deepest colours; and the wreaths, vines and forests painted on the walls faded to grey in the gloom and smoke, or blazed red, blue, green and gold if they were near the light.

Through one door came the soldiers, the executioner, the priests, the coffin and the Czarevich. And the procession stopped in astonishment, with soldiers bumping into priests, and priests stumbling back into soldiers. They stopped at the sight of the Czar-chair.

The Czarevich Safa, who didn't know how to behave at executions, even his own, wandered forward to the very foot of the Czar-chair steps. There he stopped and looked up, and he alone, of all the people in the room, seemed unalarmed.

At the other door came the sound of the Czaritsa's coal-sewn dress clashing its swinging folds together; and in marched the Czaritsa's procession.

Not a courtier, not a soldier, not a priest, glanced at their Czaritsa. Their faces were all lifted towards the Czar-chair.

The Czaritsa herself looked up at it – and stopped. Even her breathing stopped, and her great sucking of breath an instant later was heard throughout the room.

With that breath she screeched, 'You lied! You lied! *This* is the reward you wanted for bringing my nephew to me!'

For, in the Czar-chair sat Kuzma, the shaman. His hands rested on its either arm. His black and grey hair, in its badger stripes, spread over the thick, yellow-whiteness of the bearskin he wore. From the thicket of hair his sharp face peered out, whiter than the bearskin.

He looked down at the Czaritsa and said, 'I did not bring my apprentice to you, and I have come to take him from you.'

Now the Czaritsa saw Kuzma in her chair – Kuzma who had brought Safa to her – and she was outraged that he should tell such lies. Such plain lies, to her face! Her face as scarlet as the stones in her crown, she raised both clenched fists and pounded them in air. She couldn't speak for rage.

Kuzma smiled, and stood. The thick, heavy softness of the bearskin fell from the Czar-chair's seat and tumbled about the shaman's Lappish boots. Kuzma lifted his hand and beckoned to Safa, and Safa started forward to go to him.

But the Czaritsa Margaretta reached out, snatched at Safa's wrist and held it.

'Make him Czar?' she cried. 'You won't make him Czar! Executioner!'

And the executioner swung his heavy, sharp-edged axe at Safa's head, though Safa stood upright.

There was a shout from everyone in the court-room, as some struggled to turn away from the sight of the axe-blow; and some struggled to see it.

Safa started back and raised his hand, as if to protect himself from the blow – but then dropped his hand and lifted his head to meet the axe's edge. The axe dashed in his face as a slap of cold water, the drench of a wave.

The executioner stepped back and held up his empty, dripping hands. The steps, the floor, the Czaritsa, were all splattered with the salt-water spray. The Czaritsa released Safa as she spread her own wet arms and looked down in amazement at her wet dress.

Safa ran up the steps to stand beside Kuzma and wipe his wet face with his hands.

Kuzma took something from a pocket of his heavy coat and threw it down to the court-room floor. It fell with a loud noise, and rolled – it was a hard, round, smooth pebble of quartz, so hard that it could have been thrown from a much greater height without cracking or chipping. 'On that stone,' said Kuzma, 'I have spelled words. You cannot read them, you cannot see them – but until you can take these words from that stone, you can do my apprentice no harm.'

People – even the armed soldiers – began backing away from the Czar-chair and the witch, the shaman, who stood before it.

Kuzma drew the collar of his thick bearskin coat up around his neck, and set the bear's head on his own. 'As for me . . . I am already dead; so I have no fear of death.'

And Kuzma jumped down from the Czar-chair steps.

People shouted, and people laughed aloud, to see the shaman throw himself down, head-first, as if he would somersault, like an acrobat-clown.

But the shaman turned no somersaults. A man jumped from the topmost step, but a long, snake-necked bear struck the lowest step with its out-stretched legs and clawed feet.

The Czaritsa led her people – she led them in determined flight from the terrifying bear. To every door the crowds pushed in a solid, flowing band, like a rushing stream.

Every door from the court-room was blocked; and the pressing people blocked the bear's way to the Czaritsa. The bear roared.

At the roaring of the bear, courtiers, soldiers and priests pushed open the doors of rooms – any door, any room – and crowded in, slamming the doors after them.

Past the closed doors the bear ran, intent on the heels of the screeching Czaritsa – and no matter that she opened doors and slammed them after her. The thing that pursued her, though toothed and clawed like a bear, was a shaman; and no door stays closed against a shaman.

So into rooms by one door and out of them by

another ran the Czaritsa, the glassy folds of her dress clashing and ringing about her legs. And more and more, as she ran, she came upon doors that were closed and locked; and when she hammered on them for admittance, the people inside were silent and pretended they had not heard.

In one long corridor the Czaritsa fell with a thump against every door, and banged with her fist and cried, 'Let your Czaritsa in!'

And from behind the doors came the answers:

'Oh, Czaritsa, we would open the door, but the lock has jammed and we can't!'

'Oh, we are trying to open the door, Czaritsa, but it has warped in the wet and is stuck, stuck fast!'

'*I* would open the door, I *want* to open the door – but these others here won't let me!'

Before any answer was finished, the Czaritsa had seen the bear, and had run on to another door, with a crash of her jet-gown.

Pressed against the doors of those locked rooms, the hiding people listened to the passing rattle and rush of the Czaritsa's dress – and that sound and her screeches had no sooner dimmed than they heard the heavy tread of the loping bear, its claws striking on the stone floor even through the carpets, and the sigh of air through its thick fur.

And the people cowered to the floor, glad of the door between them and it, but listening eagerly for the end of the chase.

The steps of the tallest tower in the Palace were unguarded for once, all the soldiers having gone to the execution; and here the Czaritsa ran. But she could not climb the steps in her heavy gown. They were too steep, and she was too old, and had run too far already. On the steps she collapsed, and the bear came closer – and the Czaritsa sat up and faced it, and began to talk. While she talked, she went backwards up the steps on her jet-covered backside – and the bear followed, slowly now, step by step, grinning its big teeth in her face.

The Czaritsa offered the bear land, and she offered it a fortune; she offered it titles, a place in her government, a post in her army. She promised to appoint an Imperial Commission to inquire into the Czarevich's arrest and discover who was responsible. Shuffling backwards before it up the stairs, she told it every lie her tired and frightened brain could invent, and made it every offer. If it would only leave her and let her live, it could have her nephew Safa, to do whatever it liked with: if a meal was what it wanted, then it could have the choice of any of her subjects, prepared in whatever manner it chose, each day of its life. But still the bear slowly climbed the steps after her, and gave no sign of being persuaded. What else could she offer? Did the bear want a fellowship at a University? Did it fancy the captaincy of a ship? Could she bribe it with a place in the Church?

But, at last, the Czaritsa despaired of there being a human spirit in the bear. It must be a real bear, that did not understand speech – for it could not be deceived.

157

Up the steps, round and round, the bear and the Czaritsa went, to the top of the tower.

Once there, the Czaritsa ran into the dome-room, into its darkness, its windowless, imprisoning circle.

After her, through the little door, into the little room, went the big bear.

And where was there to go from there?

Nowhere, but out and down again. The bear came out, in a little while, and loped down the stairs. Behind it came rolling, falling, banging, the Czaritsa's crown; and at each bang a scarlet stone broke from the crown and lay on the dark steps, all its colour and sparkle gone. A breeze, rising and growing stronger, ruffled the bear's fur and followed it down the steps and through the corridors, rushing draughtily past closed and locked doors, lifting the fringes of carpets, shaking hangings.

In the corridors, in the jewelled light from the high windows, the bear rose upright. There were black stains about its mouth – who knew what colour those stains might have been by daylight? The bear pushed back its own head and revealed the head of Kuzma. The bear's hide fell open like a coat to show the shaman's robe beneath. The wind that had arisen with the fading of the scarlet stones still blew, tossing Kuzma's hair and beard, and growing so strong that it even lifted the heavy bearskin he wore and shook it as if it had been cloth.

Kuzma's body walked back through the Palace to the court-room, and met no one. All were in hiding.

When Kuzma's body entered the court-room, the wind entered with it, whooping round the door-posts and slapping the hangings against the painted walls. The room was empty of people, except for the Czar-chair. In that sat Safa.

Kuzma stopped at the bottom of the Czar-chair's steps and, looking up, said, 'Are you the Czar now? Is that what you wish?'

Safa said, 'Where are you going, Chingis? I want to go with you.'

'Why do you call me Chingis?' Kuzma asked.

'I can see you, Chingis! And I see Marien – and two others . . . Chingis: teach me to be a shaman.'

'To be a shaman, you must travel the ghost-world.'

'Let me go there with you!' Safa said.

'We are going there – but we won't be returning this hundred years.'

Safa rose from the Czar-chair and started down the steps. 'Whatever world you are in, Chingis, that is the world where I want to be.'

From Kuzma's coat Chingis made Kuzma's dead hand take the ice-apple. It shone and increased its shining as it gathered light. Its soothing, cold, apple-scent reached out to Safa; and hungry ice-water jetted in his mouth.

He took the apple from Kuzma's hand, but from Chingis's giving. It clung to the skin of his hand, like freezing metal.

He put it in his mouth, and it froze to his lips, and to his tongue.

He bit, and the apple shattered between his teeth with a snap, a crack, a split, like ice breaking. He swallowed winter; and followed Chingis through the gate into the ghost-world.

But what exactly became of the Czaritsa? Nothing was ever found of her except – when a lantern was taken to the dome-room – an enormous quantity of jet beads.

I am a learned cat, and I can say with authority that the digestions of shamans and white bears are strong, and able to cope with whale-meat and even small bones. But they can't cope with fossilized coal.

And the Czaritsa's spirit? Like Kuzma's, it entered the ghost-world in captivity.

What became of the Czardom, left without a Czar? What you might expect became of it. The rich and the powerful went to war, to decide who would be the next Czar.

The winner took the Czar-chair, the Palace and the crown. This new ruler was, or became, cruel, secretive, sudden, and unreasonable beyond reason. This is the nature of Czars and Czaritsas, or it is what Czardoms make them.

If the world were well rid of every Czar, then the most greedy, the most cruel, and the least truthful of those left would call themselves Czars – and the rest would let them do it.

But we need not love Czars, and we need not become them.

FIFTEEN

Now, says the cat, I must tell the end of the story. One more drop and the cup is full.

It is midwinter: the midnight of a darkness half a year long. Five hundred years have passed, but winters are still the same. A while ago the snow fell deep: now it has frozen to a sharp crust of ice. Far overhead the sky-stars glitter white, bright, in their darkness; underfoot the snow-stars glitter white in whiteness. Between the sky-stars and the snow-stars hangs a shivering, milky curtain of twilight.

In an emptiness of snow and darkness there is a village, half buried, with frost snapping and buzzing from roof to roof. In this village on Midwinter Night, in one and the same hour, five children were born.

Never before had five children been born so close in time, and the villagers were afraid. It was unnatural: they feared there was bad luck in it.

One of the babies had an old woman's grey hair to go with her newborn wrinkles; another had a thin mark on her neck, like the first cut of a blade. The villagers learned these things as they trudged over the snow from house to house. They wanted to celebrate, and drink and sing to the arrival of the new children, but instead they were forced to be sad. It was not wise to raise these children, they said. Their mothers should lay them naked on the snow and leave them to cry themselves to death.

But before any of the children were more than an hour old, another omen was seen, though whether for good or bad no one could tell. The curtain of twilight that hung from the bright stars was parted by a bobbing, pouncing light that travelled nearer and nearer.

Wrapped in shawls and blankets, the villagers stood in the snow, watching in dread and hope the thing that approached them. It brought, they felt sure, some great event – the destruction of them all, perhaps. And they could not escape.

After a long time of watching, when they were chilled and shaking, they saw that the moving lights came from the candlelit windows of a house which trotted over the snow on its cat's legs at great speed. A witch's house. A witch come to do them harm.

People stumbled on cold-stiffened legs to fetch crucifixes and knives, icons and scythes, and stood ready to defend themselves against witchcraft.

When it reached the other houses, the witch's house stopped. Mewing, it folded its legs and brought its door close to the ground. The doors opened and out came an old woman, dressed in the outlandish manner of a shaman.

She laughed at the saints' pictures and crosses the villagers held towards her. 'I haven't come to hurt you tonight,' she shouted. 'I've come for the children who were born here an hour ago. Wrap them well and bring them here!'

And the old witch sat on her doorstep, holding her staff between her knees.

The villagers ran, scattering into the houses and returning in five jostling groups, each with a woman at their centre, carrying a baby wrapped in whatever shawl, or shirt, or rag had come to hand.

The first to be carried up to the witch was the grey-haired baby. 'My sister,' said the witch, and took the baby and kissed it. Gently she laid the baby on the floor of her house, and turned to see the next.

This second baby she also kissed, saying, 'That one was married to a Czar. May her luck be better this time! – Let me see that other child!'

The third baby was put into the crook of the witch's other arm, while her carved staff stood upright by itself. 'Ah, yes,' said the witch, '*this* one once nursed a Czar's child. May she meet no Czars and nurse her own children!' And the witch sang an old, old song and sang the babies to sleep. 'Take these two back,' she said. 'Don't fear them; they have nothing of the witch about them, but they will be fortunate in their lives – Give me the others! They are the children I've travelled to find.'

When the last two babies, a girl and a boy, were put into her arms, she said, 'Yes! This is the little witch who will soon be teaching me – and this is the

Czar's son whose birth has been luckier than before. These, and my sister, I shall take into my keeping and out of your knowing.'

The witch rose and carried the two babies into the hut, where the first already lay, and she closed her door on the villagers. The hut rose on its cat's legs and made its jerky, jumping way over the snow until the shimmering, flickering curtain of star-shine and twilight closed over it and wiped it from their eyes.

The villagers remembered the night for centuries; but never saw a witch again. And of those witches who choose to take no interest in the short lives of ordinary men and women, what can even such a learned cat as I tell? I dare know nothing of them; I dare tell nothing of their ways – but now he is a shaman and not a Czarevich, I think there are no doors closed against Safa that he cannot open.

The babies left behind in the village were given the names Farida and Marien. They grew in the usual slow way; they were loved, and lived lives of such ordinary peace, of such ordinary hardship, of such unremarkable loss, gain and happiness, that I can only wonder at such a miracle, and find nothing more to tell of them.

But the spirits of Kuzma and Margaretta were carried, imprisoned, into the ghost-world. Did they return to this world again?

I will tell you, says the cat, of a place in this Czardom I speak of, where rusty stone is broken from the earth; and smashed; and heated; and from the heated stone runs molten iron.

This iron is used to make every kind of tool — hammers, for instance. Every size of hammer.

There was once a blacksmith who bought two of the biggest hammers, two great fists of iron, and had them carried to his forge in a wagon.

At the centre of the blacksmith's forge stood an anvil, made of iron from the ground beneath the blacksmith's feet. The blacksmith loved the anvil. It was his work-table and his seat. Its horns and its holes shaped his work. Without it, he wouldn't have been a blacksmith.

He fixed his new hammers over the anvil on long, springy poles of ashwood. A tarred rope tied the ash-poles to see-saw planks on the floor. When the blacksmith rocked the planks with his feet, down came the hammers – kang! pang! on the anvil – and flew up into the rafters again.

The blacksmith grew to love his new hammers. They were so obedient to him. When he had work on his anvil, he had only to touch his foot to the see-saw planks and – k-rang! dang! dang! – the hammers willingly beat their heads on the iron for him. He loved their tin-pots-and-pans singing as they danced together, passing each other by in mid-air. He came to think that, when his work was good, it was because his clever hammers had worked so hard to help him, forgetting that they only worked because he made them. He grew so fond of them that he gave them names. The names slipped into his head, and he didn't know why he thought of those particular names, but the hammer on the right he called 'Margaretta', and the other he called 'Kuzma'. To the singing of the hammers he called out their names – 'Come down, Kuzma! Down, Margie! Kuzma! Margie!'

To the anvil he gave no name, though he would often affectionately follow its shape with his hand. The anvil never moved, and so never seemed alive.

Every day, the hammer Margaretta, and the hammer Kuzma worked. Every day, every week, every month, every year, they beat their heads on the iron the blacksmith shaped. Often the smith's children would hop on and off the planks, and make the hammers leap and ring for a game.

On the day of the blacksmith's death, the hammers were made to ring a carillon on the anvil as a mark of respect – and the next day, the blacksmith's son set them hammering to earn his keep.

They lasted to sing their tin-pots song for the son of the blacksmith's son too, but nothing lasts for ever. On the same day, at the same moment, both hammers cracked and broke.

The anvil had stood and received their blows, with no means of returning them; but in the end the anvil always outlasts the hammers.

The spirits of hammer Margaretta and of hammer Kuzma flew free to the ghost-world. Had their years of labour, the hammering of their heads, their breaking on the anvil, taught them anything, or made them change in their iron natures?

Not by one whit. Iron may be pitted, broken,

rusted, twisted – but it is never anything but iron.

And that is the end of the story, says the cat. It was all true – I know it was true, because I was at the Czaritsa's funeral and wet my whiskers in the beer drunk there. They haven't dried yet.
Open the windows and let the lies fly out!

If you thought this story tasty, then serve it to others, says the cat.
If you thought it sour, then sweeten it with your own telling.
But whether you liked it, or liked it not, take it away and let it make its own way back to me, riding on another's tongue.

The cat lays herself down among the links of her golden chain and tucks her forepaws beneath her breast. Head up, ears pricked, she falls asleep under her oak-tree, and neither sings nor tells stories.